STAR WARS

REBEL ✦ FORCE

RENEGADE

BY ALEX WHEELER

LUCAS BOOKS

SCHOLASTIC INC.

New York   Toronto   London   Auckland   Sydney   Mexico City   New Delhi   Hong Kong   Buenos Aires

ISBN-13: 978-0-545-11211-6
ISBN-10: 0-545-11211-7

12 11 10 9 8 7 6 5 4 3 2 1   9 10 11 12 13/0

Book design by Rick DeMonico
Cover illustration by Randy Martinez

Printed in the U.S.A.
First printing, May 2009

The blue beam lit up the night, slashing through the darkness with an eerie glow. It painted swooping circles of light through the still air, the brilliant blue dancing to the music of chittering chucklucks and warbling bellybirds. Then, suddenly, the beam went out.

The darkness was complete.

Luke Skywalker stood motionless in the shadows of the towering Massassi trees, his hand gripped tightly around the lightsaber's hilt, waiting.

For what, he didn't know.

There were times when the lightsaber seemed to illuminate the world. Wielding the Jedi weapon made him feel safe and in control, as if the warm, blue glow kindled something inside of him. The lightsaber had been his father's, and it was his only true connection to the man who had been dead for as long as Luke could remember.

Times like these, he felt like a true Jedi. Like he was joined with the Force that Obi-Wan had told him about, surrounding him, penetrating him. He was filled with a cool certainty that the Force would guide his way. That the lightsaber was more than a connection to his father. It was a connection to his destiny.

Then there were the other times. Times when the darkness overpowered the light.

Luke had spent the last several hours in the heart of the jungle, training with his lightsaber and trying to ignore his growing sense of dread. There could be nothing to fear on a night like this. The tropical humidity of Yavin 4 had given way to an unusually balmy evening. Massassi leaves rustled in the cool breeze, and in the distance, Luke could hear the muffled shouts of a casual game of zoneball. Inspired by the weather, the Rebels had come alive, engaging in landspeeder races, pick-up Grav-ball games, and parties. As if no one sensed the dark clouds on the horizon, the air heavy with doom.

Clearly none of them did, except for Luke, who suspected he was imagining things. Searching for problems where none existed. And so, unable to sweat out his tension in lightsaber training, he abandoned the calisthenics. On a night like this, there was only one sure way to cast off the unwanted tension — to escape all his problems, real and imaginary, giving in to the sheer joy of speed.

The speeder bikes were parked near the living quarters. Princess Leia Organa waved at him through the window as he passed, then turned back to her conversation with Han Solo. Although Luke couldn't hear them through the transparisteel, he could easily guess what they were doing: arguing.

It was pretty much all they ever did.

For a moment, he thought about going inside to break up the fight. But instead, he continued toward his bike. It was too nice a night to spend cooped up inside. He knew that trapped between four walls, his anxiety would likely boil over. He needed to be out in the wild, riding fast and free.

Tobin Elad, one of the newest recruits to the Rebel cause, was leaning against the crusty, purple bark of a crooked Massassi tree, watching the planet Yavin dip beneath the horizon. The night blazed orange as the massive gas giant plunged through the clouds. "Nice weather for a ride," Elad said, nodding as Luke passed.

The darkness was back. Stronger than ever. Luke forced a weak smile, fighting off the nausea. "Want to join me?"

Elad shook his head. "Another time," he said. "But have a good one."

Luke climbed aboard the bike, eager to get started. The speeders could go more than 500 kilometers an hour — surely fast enough to outrun the darkness.

He turned the ignition. The engine roared to life.

And everything froze.

For Luke, time slowed nearly to a stop, and everything became frighteningly clear. The burnt umber of the sky, the humid kiss of the wind. The vibrations of the speeder bike beneath him. The certainty that something was terribly, terribly wrong. This wasn't darkness he could outrun or ignore. This wasn't his imagination.

This was a warning.

As time sped into motion again, Luke flung himself from the speeder. He didn't think, he just acted, launching himself into the air — as the bike exploded in a ball of blue-gold fire.

X-7 didn't feel, not in the normal human sense.

But as Luke's body slammed into the ground, limbs bent at odd, awkward angles, as the raging fire crept toward his still, broken form, X-7 allowed himself a small smile. There was nothing like the satisfaction of a job well done.

Then he saw Luke's chest rise and fall.

His smile disappeared.

X-7, the man Luke knew as Tobin Elad, rushed to kneel beside the body. If anyone was watching, it would look like the loyal Elad was desperate to save his fallen friend. No one would see the assassin's hand covering Luke's mouth, his fingers pinching Luke's nose shut, the feeble flailing of a wounded body struggling to breathe. Just a few more seconds, and his mission would be complete. Luke Skywalker, destroyer of the Death Star, hope of the Rebellion, target of the Empire's most ruthless assassin, would finally be —

"*Luuuuuuke!*"

X-7 winced as Leia's screech pierced the night. He had only a split second to decide — kill Luke now, once and for all, and risk discovery? Or let the situation play itself out.

He let his hand drop away from Luke's nose and mouth. Within moments, a panicked crowd had formed around the fallen Rebel. "The bike just exploded," X-7 said, as Leia cradled Luke's head in her lap, urging him to hold on until the medical droids arrived. Han Solo appeared just behind her, hands clenched in frustration at not being able to act. "It's lucky he wasn't killed instantly."

Lucky indeed. The speeder had been wired with enough explosives to blow Luke's body to bits — but that was assuming Luke had stayed on the bike. Instead, he'd thrown himself out of the way, just in time.

How did he know? X-7 thought, frustrated.

Not that it mattered. The shock wave had caught him, flung him like a rag doll. And if Luke's current injuries didn't kill him, X-7 would help them along. Nothing was easier than taking down weakened prey.

Three 2-1B medical droids loaded Luke onto a stretcher and carried him away, their prongs and manipulator arms already at work assessing the damage. As the fire burned itself out, the crowd lingered, reluctant to leave the scene.

"Could it have been an accident?" Leia asked, looking anxiously in the direction the droids had taken Luke.

Han and X-7 shook their heads at the same time. "Someone sabotaged that bike," X-7 said grimly. "No doubt."

"But who'd want to hurt the kid?" Han said.

X-7 held in another small smile. Han was about to get his answer.

They all were.

This is wrong, Leia thought, waiting impatiently for the Rebel security patrol to bring her some kind of answers. Yavin 4 was supposed to be a stronghold, a safe base for the Rebel Alliance. *Alliance* was the key word. They were supposed to all be on the same side. Fighting the Empire, not each other.

But somehow, an enemy had found his or her way into the heart of the Rebellion. And now Luke was immersed in a bath of healing bacta, fighting for his life; the enemy was still out there somewhere. And Leia was just waiting. Helpless.

Useless.

General Dodonna and Commander Willard had convened a hasty tribunal to investigate the crime and prosecute the would-be assassin — if he or she could be found. Leia would have chosen General Airen Cracken to head the investigation, but she had to admit, the

7

leader of Alliance Intelligence had bigger things to worry about. Which meant Leia would have to do the job herself.

"Report," she ordered Lieutenant Fraj T'lin, whom she'd tasked with beginning the field work while she hovered anxiously by Luke's bacta tank. T'lin flinched, like he was afraid she would lash out. Leia sighed, forcing herself to be patient. She was exhausted and frustrated, not a good combination. After the explosion, the medical droids had struggled to keep Luke alive through the night. He made it through to sunrise, but it had taken nearly another full day and night to stabilize him. A full day and night that Leia had sat beside his unconscious, broken body, silently begging him to live. And wondering what she would do if he died.

She hadn't slept. How could she, when Luke was fighting to survive?

How could she sleep now, when the assassin was still out there?

"Well?" she snapped, when T'lin seemed reluctant to speak. "Have you uncovered anything?"

The lieutenant, an Arpor-Lan, tugged nervously at the stubby horns sprouting from his chin. "We released our modified patrol droids throughout the compound. Each is capable of detecting traces of detonite through more than two meters of durasteel or any other protective casing."

Leia forced herself to be patient. T'lin was babbling, and she wanted to shake him, force him to get to the point. But she had to remind herself that the explosion had come as a nasty surprise to everyone. They were all rattled. They were all doing their best.

Including the enemy, Leia thought. *He's doing his best, too. To kill Luke. And he almost succeeded.*

"And your droids found something . . . ?" she prompted T'lin.

He cleared his throat. "Maybe it's better you see for yourself."

Leia rolled her eyes, but she agreed to follow him. The lieutenant brought her down the path toward the living quarters, then wove through the buildings to a familiar door.

"What are we doing here?" Leia asked, beginning to understand why Lieutenant T'lin was refusing to meet her gaze.

"Through here, Your Highness," he said in response, ushering her into the room.

While on Yavin 4, Han Solo spent most of his time on the *Millennium Falcon*. No reason to put down roots, he always said. After all, it's not like he was joining the Rebellion.

He'd always refused to do that.

Still, the ship was cramped, rusted, and falling apart. And when he tired of tinkering with cracked transducer panels or leaky fuel conduits, the sparsely furnished room offered Han a place to stretch out and relax with a good game of dejarik.

The room was empty now, except for a rusted patrol droid. Like most of the Rebellion's equipment, the droids had been scavenged from abandoned Imperial outposts and retrofitted for service to the Alliance. This one, equipped with a highly sensitive modified sensor array, hovered next to a low cabinet, whirring urgently.

The door was half-open, offering a glimpse inside. Leia caught her breath.

"Is that . . . ?" she said when she was able to speak.

Lieutenant T'lin nodded, looking surer of himself, now that she could see the evidence for herself. "Two kilos of detonite. Enough to blow half this base sky-high. Who knows what he was planning to do with the rest of it."

"He wouldn't have," Leia said. "He couldn't have."

"I know he's a friend, Your Highness —"

"Where is he?" she snapped, remembering herself. She forced the emotion out of her voice and off her face. "Have you confronted him with this?"

"Denied it was his," T'lin said flatly. "Claims he was framed. Got no proof, though."

Of course he was framed, she reassured herself. *Han would never betray us. He would never hurt Luke.*

"How well do you really know him?" the lieutenant asked.

"Well enough," she said tersely. "I presume you've taken him into custody?"

"He's waiting to be interrogated," T'lin said. "We assumed you'd want to select someone for the job."

"You assumed right," she said. "I'll do it myself."

"You don't think he could have done it?" Tobin Elad half-said, half-asked, as they stood outside the room where Han was being held. Though she'd only known him a short time, he'd become a good friend.

Of course, that's what she would have said about Han, too.

Nothing's changed, she told herself. *Han didn't do this.*

Leia shook her head. "I know Han. Someone must have set him up."

Elad nodded. "It could have been anyone." He gave her a wry smile. "Maybe you should be interrogating me," he suggested. "After all, I just showed up out of nowhere, right? You barely know me."

"You showed up out of nowhere and saved all our lives," she reminded him. "And you joined the Rebellion as soon as you had the chance. You've been with us every step of the way."

"Just like Han," Elad pointed out.

"Han refuses to join us," Leia pointed out. "He claims the only cause he believes in is the cause of himself."

"He's a good liar."

"Yes. . . ." Leia said thoughtfully. "He is."

"I know Han brags about being willing to do anything for money," Elad said, "and that he's always reminding us that the Rebellion isn't his fight, but *you* know him, Leia. You know who he really is."

Leia knew Elad had been trying to comfort her. To assure her that Han was innocent. And she *knew* that to be the case. Deep down, she felt it. Han was a good man, a loyal man.

But with every word out of Elad's mouth, she found herself more and more uncertain. How well *did* she know Han? How much of what came out of his mouth was bluster — and how much was true? He boasted about being a mercenary, loyal to no one but himself.

Empty boasts, she reminded herself.

Maybe.

"You want me to go in there with you?" Elad asked.

She didn't want to face Han alone. She didn't want to face him at all, not with these accusations hanging over him. But Luke's life was at stake — perhaps all their lives. "I need to do this myself," she said.

She had to find out what was really going on, and right now, Han was her only lead. This wasn't about what she wanted. It was about being objective. Yes, she would give Han every chance in the world to establish his innocence. But in the end, she wasn't here as his friend. She was here as a representative of the Rebel Alliance Tribunal, and that meant she needed more than just her gut instinct that Han was innocent.

She needed proof.

Han didn't know how the explosives had ended up in his quarters. He didn't know who would want to frame him. He didn't know what the Rebels would do if they didn't believe his story, and he didn't know how long they thought they could hold him in this dank cell, asking him question after question.

But he did know who they'd send in to get their answers.

He knew she wouldn't be able to resist.

"Greetings, Your Worshipfulness," he said wryly, as she stepped into the room. "Fancy meeting a princess like you in a place like this."

She scowled. "Luke is doing better, if you care," she said.

As if there was any doubt that he cared.

"You seen him yet?" Han asked, careful to keep his voice neutral. He wasn't about to go all weepy over the kid, especially now that he knew Luke would be all right. Sure, he'd been worried, but Luke was tough. Certainly tougher than Han had expected, the first time they'd met. Just like that old hermit of his — both of them proving more than met the eye.

Of course, tough hadn't been enough to keep the old man alive.

Luke's fine, he reminded himself. *Worry about yourself. And Chewie.*

The room, really a large closet in the rear corridor of a storage facility, was completely bare, except for two chairs. Han was sprawled in a corner, doing his best to look comfortable and unconcerned. But when Leia sat down in one of the chairs and pointed to the other one, he gave in and took a seat.

"I don't know anything about those explosives," he said, getting down to business. "Someone's setting me up."

"You have proof?" Leia asked. She sounded almost skeptical.

Which was impossible, because of all people, Leia had to know he'd never hurt Luke. . . . right?

"You want me to *prove* someone's setting me up?" Han asked. "How am I supposed to prove anything, locked in here?"

She didn't answer. "Who do you think it might be?" she asked.

"I don't *know*," he said, frustrated. "But it's obviously got to be someone."

"Because?"

"Because it wasn't *me*," he snapped. "Why would I try to kill the kid?"

Leia raised her eyebrows. "Why do you do anything?"

"I don't believe this!" Han exclaimed. "What kind of laserbrain does it take to think that *I* would go after Luke?"

He expected her temper to flare, as it always did. They would argue, as they always did, and in the end, she wouldn't be able to stop herself from laughing, as she always did. Then they would agree that this was insane and get to work on finding the real culprit.

Except she didn't take the bait. And when she spoke, her voice was level and perfectly calm. Only then did he start to worry. "I don't know why anyone would go after Luke," she said. "But someone did."

"You really believe I could do this?" It looked bad — he knew that. Explosives in Han's quarters, explosives on Luke's bike. Even a nerf-brain could draw the connection. But Leia was no nerf-brain, which meant she should have been able to see that the connection was *too* obvious. This wasn't just a frame-up job, it was a *bad* frame-up job.

It was almost like she didn't want to see it — like she *wanted* him to be guilty.

"I'm just trying to be objective," Leia said. "Evaluate the evidence, find the truth. My personal beliefs don't enter into it."

"Okay, let's say I did it," he said, trying a different tack. "Why would I be stupid enough to hide the explosives in my quarters? Why not on my ship? Or in someone else's?"

"Why would someone set you up?" Leia countered. "You barely know anyone here."

"Because I'm not a part of the Rebellion, you mean?" Han said. "That's what this is about, isn't it?"

"That's not —"

"After all the times I've saved your skin, you still don't trust me, because I won't put on a uniform and sign on the dotted line."

"I'm just asking questions, Han."

"And I'm done answering them." Han folded his arms. "After everything I've done for you and your Rebellion, you suspect me of —" He shook his head. "No."

Leia leaned forward. "If you're innocent, Han, help me prove it. Help me help you."

But there it was: *if.*

She didn't trust him. After all they'd been through. "You know, I'd never accuse *you* of something like this," he pointed out.

"That's different," she said.

"Yeah. I guess it is." Han stood up and returned to the dark corner he'd been lounging in when she arrived. "I guess we're done here."

"This isn't over," Leia warned him. "It's my job to get to the bottom of this."

"Fine." Han couldn't look at her. "But it's not my job to help you."

She still didn't betray a hint of emotion, nothing to indicate there was anything between them but unanswered questions. She didn't even slam the door on her way out.

But she still locked it.

ey, you can't go in there!" The guard
backed up against the wall of the
makeshift brig, blaster in one hand,
comlink in the other. He was clearly
undecided about what he should do first: call for reinforcements or shoot. "This is your last warning, you
hairy — *oof*."

With a single, furry blow to the head, Chewbacca
saved him the trouble of deciding. The Wookiee
slammed the blaster into the wall, then crushed the
comlink under his massive foot. The guard would be
fine when he woke up. He just wouldn't wake up any
time soon.

These humans were so fragile. Sometimes it seemed
even a sneeze would knock them over.

A Wookiee sneeze, at least.

Chewbacca was a Wookiee of many loyalties. But
none was greater than the loyalty he owed to the human

who'd saved his life back on Kashyyyk. Ever since, when Han Solo called, Chewbacca delivered.

And that night, as Yavin's many moons crawled across the sky, the call had come: "Get me out of here, Chewie!"

Chewbacca planned to deliver.

Han was being kept in the back room of a supply warehouse. Once past the Rebel guarding the door, Chewbacca thudded down the hallway. His bulk made stealth impossible; his strength made it unnecessary.

"Stop the Wookiee!" someone shouted from behind him.

"Don't kill him!" came another voice. "Just stun him!"

The blaster fire came fast and heavy. Though he knew it wouldn't be lethal, Chewbacca dodged and weaved, ducking the explosions. A few glanced off his thick hide, but it took more than a single stun blast to put down a Wookiee. Still, he had to find some cover. The guards were calling for reinforcements — soon he'd be even more outnumbered and the rescue mission would be ruined.

He couldn't let Han down.

Chewbacca ducked behind the nearest obstacle he could find, a giant durasteel cart brimming with the disgusting protein supplements the humans ate for many of their meals. Laserfire raked the side of the cart, scorching the durasteel and sending sparks flying into the smoky air, but Chewbacca was safe for the moment. He peeked over the top of the cart. There were only four humans, now standing abreast in the hallway, blocking his path to Han.

The cart was on wheels.

Chewbacca had seen the facilities workers wheeling these carts to the kitchen — it took three humans to inch them slowly to the repulsorlift conveyor belts that would distribute the food. The Wookiee pressed one hairy shoulder against the cart and pushed it forward with ease. He heaved it down the hallway. The guards scattered, but not quickly enough. Humans and blasters went flying, as the metal beast mowed them down in their path. In the confusion, Chewbacca snatched their blasters out of the air, tucking two into his bandolier and shattering the other two with a single sharp crack against the wall.

Even the most foolish human wouldn't face down a Wookiee without weapons. The four men cowered against the wall, hands in the air. Chewbacca pointed at one of their comlinks and growled.

No one moved.

Humans could be so dense sometimes. Chewbacca pulled out his own comlink, miming talking into it, then pointed at the door on the far side of the hall.

One of the guards nodded quickly. "I think he wants

us to call off the reinforcements," he told the others in a squeaky voice. "Done." He raised his comlink. "Uh, false alarm over here at the brig," he said, shakily. "All's well with the prisoner. Facility is secure." Then he gave Chewbacca a hopeful grin. "That okay, boy?" he asked, speaking slowly and enunciating clearly, as if Chewbacca was a rather large and rather stupid pet.

Don't hurt anyone you don't have to, Han had said.

Chewbacca sighed. And instead of whacking the human over the head, he knotted the four guards together with their own binders. Then he hurried to the end of the hall to retrieve his best friend.

The door was locked. But when Chewbacca pounded a massive fist against it, the thin plastoid crumbled like flimsiplast. Han was already on his feet. Chewbacca tossed his friend a blaster. "Took you long enough!" Han complained, heading for the open door.

Chewbacca growled.

"Yeah, yeah, you did fine, Chewie," Han admitted. "Now — you want a medal, or you want to get out of here?"

Apparently, the Alliance had kept its suspicions of Han under wraps. Because when he and Chewie swept into the main hangar deck, the deck officers on duty just waved him a sleepy hello. They were used to seeing

Han and Chewbacca tinkering with the *Falcon* at all hours of the night, and blasting into orbit for the occasional emergency mission. The Alliance had instituted a strict departure protocol, but Han wasn't much for protocols, and everyone knew it.

"Requesting permission for departure!" he shouted, winking as he ran past the senior deck officer. The officer, barely more than a kid, flushed with pleasure at the friendly gesture. No one but the newest, greenest recruits got stuck with the overnight shift. And all of the newest, greenest recruits craved attention from Han Solo.

"Permission granted," the kid shouted back, grinning. Han and Chewbacca hurtled toward the ship, strapped themselves in, and threw themselves into the takeoff protocol. With a thunder of engines and a cloud of black steam from a broken exhaust port, the *Millennium Falcon* was in the air.

The Corellian freighter might not have looked too pretty, but she could take off in a hurry when she had to.

As she often did.

"*Millennium Falcon*, this is base. Return to surface immediately."

Han ignored the request.

"Repeat, *Millennium Falcon*, *return to base*. You are *not cleared* to leave the system."

"Ready to fire up the hyperdrive, Chewie?" Han asked, as the comlink blared with increasingly hysterical commands. He just needed to get a little farther from the moon, and then he could engage the hyperdrive and never look back.

"Captain Solo, this is General Leia Organa. Return to base immediately. This is an order."

"You didn't say pretty please, *General*," Han growled at the console.

"Land the ship immediately, Han, or we'll be forced to take extreme measures —"

Han flicked off the comlink. "How many times do I have to tell you, lady? *No one* tells me where to fly my ship."

Chewbacca let out an alarmed bark.

"They're bluffing!" Han exclaimed. "They would never —" The ship shuddered beneath them as an alarm began to blare. Han peered incredulously at a squadron of X-wing fighters that had just become visible in the cockpit window.

Chewbacca yelped.

"I *know* they're firing at us!" Han snapped. "Well, what are you waiting for? Evasive maneuvers!" Han didn't want to fire back at the Rebel ships. He probably knew some of the guys flying those X-wings, and he didn't want to hurt them.

Not unless I have to, he promised himself.

Not unless they make me.

Two of the X-wings peeled off from their formation and angled toward the *Falcon*. Laserfire streaked through space, peppering the hull. The shields held — but they wouldn't for long. Han took the ship into a steep dive, then veered to port full throttle, hoping to get below the X-wings. But the small ships were too maneuverable, and they shadowed him every step of the way.

"Engage hyperdrive!" Han shouted, as a blast slammed into the primary sensor array. "Let's get out of here." They weren't shooting to kill, but they were still shooting, and sooner or later, he was going to have to shoot back. And if it came to that . . . well, there was no way he could ever return to Yavin 4.

Not that I'm ever going back, Han reminded himself, as the ship bucked and shuddered beneath him. *Not ever.* Another volley of laserfire streaked toward them, and Han steered the ship into a 360° loop, aiming straight for the X-wings. They scattered at the last minute, darting out of his way, but quickly swiveling around to take aim at the starboard shield projector.

"Why aren't we in hyperspace yet?" Han growled.

Chewbacca yelped in alarm.

"Whaddaya *mean* it's not working?" Han asked,

glaring at the temperamental hyperdrive controls. "Weren't you supposed to fix that?"

Chewbacca barked angrily.

"I *know* you had to come rescue me," Han admitted. "It's called multitasking."

The Wookiee snorted, then turned back to the tangled nest of frayed wiring that controlled their ship's hyperdrive. He warned Han that getting it up and running could take several minutes. "We don't *have* several minutes," Han snarled. A barrage of laserfire raked across the ship. There was a spurt of fire from the port dorsal engine. A couple more hits like that and the engines would cut out all together, leaving them dead in space like a sitting kaadu. "We may not even have several *seconds!*" Han whacked the hyperdrive controls in frustration.

There was a soft whirring noise, and then the darkness of space flashed blinding white. Stars streamed past the window, twinkling points stretching to long, glowing strands that turned the galaxy into a tunnel of light. "Huh," Han said, staring in surprise at the palm of his hand. "Guess I should have tried that sooner."

They had entered hyperspace; they were safe.

Safe from the Rebel Alliance, Han thought sourly. *Never thought I'd be on the run from* them.

They flew for several long moments in silence. Then, finally, Han couldn't stand it anymore. "Go ahead," he ordered Chewbacca. "Say it."

The Wookiee barked innocently.

"You know what," Han said, leaning back in his seat. A drop of grease from the leaking cooling tubes splattered onto his head. He'd been planning to repair the thing later that week.

Maybe this was all for the best, he told himself. He'd gotten too comfortable, hanging around with Luke and Leia, pretending he was one of them. He'd gone soft.

Chewbacca was still playing dumb.

"C'mon, say what you've been thinking ever since we left the moon," Han urged him, irritably. He could tell when the Wookiee was holding out on him. "Go on; get it off your big, hairy chest."

Chewbacca sighed, then growled.

"Well, I couldn't very well protect Luke from the inside of a jail cell, could I?" Han retorted.

Chewbacca growled again.

"No, I don't know how I can help him from up here, either, fuzzbrain. I do know that if I don't pay back Jabba, I'm not going to be helping anyone any time soon. Hard to help when you're dead," Han said, groaning at the thought of how angry the Hutt crime lord must be by now. "We've wasted too much time playing war games. We need to rack up some credits. And in the meantime, if we happen to dig up something that'll help Luke —"

Chewbacca cut in with an insistent yowl.

"Why should I care about clearing my name?" Han scoffed. "They want to think I'm a traitor, after all I've done for them? Let 'em."

The Wookiee hooted.

"Leia?" Han forced a laugh. "Why would I care what Her Royal Worshipfulness thinks of me?"

Chewbacca opened his mouth as if to disagree, but Han had had enough. "Just fly the ship, will ya?"

I didn't turn my back on Leia or the Rebellion, he reminded himself, taking an inventory of all the instruments that had been damaged by the Rebel attack. *They turned their backs on* me.

Light.
Noise.
Pain.
Dark.

This was Luke's reality. He opened his eyes, grasped at a familiar voice, a face, *something* to hold onto, that would keep him from drifting away. But he could never hold tight enough; life was a jumble of sound and color that made no sense. He didn't know where he was; he barely knew *who* he was. He was a body that breathed, a body that hurt. And then his eyes would shut and the darkness would claim him again. A body that slept.

Time had no meaning in the world of pain. It could have been hours, it could have been years.

And then it was over. He opened his eyes, and he was returned to himself. And she was waiting for him.

"Easy," Leia said quietly, as Luke struggled to sit up. "You need to rest."

"What happened?" Luke croaked, his throat dry and cracked. But even as he spoke, he was remembering: the speeder. The explosion.

The dark warning from somewhere inside of him — or from outside? From the *Force*? The warning that had saved his life.

"Someone tried to kill you, Luke," Leia said. "If you hadn't jumped off that speeder when you did . . ."

"Old Ben was right," Luke murmured, amazed. *"Let go of your conscious self and act on instinct."*

"What?"

"Nothing. Just something an old friend once told me." Gingerly, Luke tested out his arms, his legs. All seemed to be in working order.

"You were injured in the blast," Leia explained, "but you've been immersed in bacta for the last few days, and you're making a full recovery. Everything should be back to normal soon."

There was a strange look in her eyes. Luke didn't understand it, but he knew that nothing was back to normal. "What aren't you telling me?"

She rested her hand on his. "Later," she said. "When you're stronger."

She was always trying to protect him. But he was stronger than she thought.

To prove it, Luke pushed himself into a sitting position. He swallowed hard, and when he spoke, his voice was clear. "Who set the explosives?" he asked. "Has the Empire attacked?" But as soon as he said it, he knew that made no sense. Nobody understood why Imperial forces hadn't yet attacked Yavin 4. But if the Empire had decided it was time to act, surely they wouldn't mess around with the death of a single pilot. They would destroy the base, and every living being on it.

But if not Imperial agents, then who?

"We're still investigating," Leia said.

"But you know something," Luke pushed, unsure why he was so certain. Was it because he just knew Leia well enough to see behind her mask? Or was it the Force again, guiding him toward the truth?

She held his gaze for a long moment, then nodded. "A cache of explosives was located . . . in Han's quarters."

"Then he was framed!" Luke exclaimed. "Han would never try to hurt me."

"That's what I thought, too," Leia said.

Thought. Past tense.

Luke shook his head. "You *can't* think —"

"I wanted to clear his name," Leia said. "I was just trying to get some information, so we'd have a place to start, but he's such a worrt-headed, hot-tempered —" She pressed her lips together, then lowered her gaze. "He broke out of custody," she said. "The *Falcon* lifted off without clearance and entered hyperspace. He's gone."

"But . . ." Luke trailed off, speechless.

". . . why would an innocent man run? That's what General Dodonna said when I informed him. Maybe it's my fault." Leia gave herself a little shake, as if she was trying to slough off her doubts about Han — or maybe her loyalty to him. "Either way, he won't be back anytime soon, not after the sendoff he got." She scowled in frustration. "I told those pilots just to *warn* him, not to *fire.*"

"Rebel pilots attacked *Han*?" Luke yelped, lurching upright so quickly that a wave of dizziness swept over him. Leia put out a hand to steady him, but he shook her off. "Is he . . . ?"

"He's fine," Leia assured him. "That ship may be a bucket of bolts, but he can still outfly anyone he —" She stopped abruptly, looking angry at herself. "Han's fine," she said brusquely. "*You're* the one in danger. And if Han didn't set those explosives —"

"He didn't," Luke cut in.

"Then whoever did is still out there," she said. "Someone's after you, Luke, and for all we know, they're going to keep coming after you until you're dead. We have to get you out of here."

"You want me to run away?" Luke asked incredulously.

"Just until we get to the bottom of this," Leia said. "Think about it — we can't trust *anyone*."

"But —"

"The Rebel Alliance *needs* you, Luke." Leia held herself very still and upright, as she often did when she was trying to cover up some personal weakness. "You're too valuable to lose. Luke — please."

That was as close as she would ever come to begging him, Luke knew, and he couldn't stand to see it. "Okay," he agreed. "Under two conditions."

"What?"

"First, you come with me."

"I'm needed here!" Leia protested.

"If I'm in danger, you could be, too," Luke reasoned. "And I'm not leaving you here to face that alone."

"What's the second condition?" Leia asked, in a weary tone that made it clear she would give in.

For the first time since waking up, Luke smiled. "*I get to pick where we go.*"

*   *   *

Pathetic, X-7 thought, approaching the room where Luke was recuperating. There were no guards, no droids, nothing. As if two sentries posted at the entrance of the medcenter would be enough to keep their most valuable patient safe. Certainly, they wouldn't be enough to keep him safe from X-7, who was waved along with a nod and a friendly grin.

These Rebels, so trusting.

So stupid.

X-7 reached into his pocket and wrapped his hand around the jet injector. Less than four centimeters long, it fit snugly in the palm of his hand. When X-7 placed a hand on his wounded friend's shoulder, no holocam would catch the tiny pinprick, the injection of two milliliters of Sennari, a toxin with lethal effects.

Sennari usually killed within seconds, but for situations like this, X-7 preferred to use a slow-acting variant of the poison. Luke would fade away in the night, long after X-7 had left the room. As the toxin was absorbed, organs would shut down, one by one. Within hours, the toxin would disappear from Luke's bloodstream, undetectable by even the most expert doctors. Luke's total system failure would appear a natural process. Unfortunate, unavoidable.

By morning, Luke would be dead.

And everyone would believe it was due to injuries sustained in the explosion.

Making Han Solo a murderer.

It had been frustrating to watch Luke survive the explosion, but maybe it was for the best, X-7 decided. Toxins were his preferred method of killing. Simple, direct — almost elegant. And no chance of error or escape.

X-7 prepared a suitably genial smile, in case Luke was awake. He opened the door.

A wave of rage crested over him, nearly knocking him off his feet. He was unused to such strong emotions. He was supposed to be *beyond* them. But it was impossible to remain calm.

The bed was empty.

The target — the weak, young, naive, *pathetic* target — was gone.

Which meant X-7 had failed again.

CHAPTER FOUR

Luke landed the shuttle on a desolate stretch of sand, several kilometers from the nearest outpost of civilization. Of course, on Tatooine, "civilization" was a relative term.

"Are you quite certain that this is the best hiding spot for us, Master Luke?" The protocol droid C-3PO tottered out of the ship, followed by his astromech counterpart, R2-D2. He stood with his hands on his hips, glaring at the bleak desert landscape. They had landed at the edge of the Dune Sea, a sandy, windswept plain that stretched to the horizon. Bleached nearly white by the harsh Tatooine suns, the ocean of sand melded seamlessly into the pale, hazy sky. "This climate is dreadfully bad for my joints!"

R2-D2 beeped gleefully, wheeling circles around his golden friend, as Leia stretched.

"Easy for you to say," C-3PO snapped. "You don't

have to worry about your language circuits getting sand-clogged. I still don't understand why we couldn't hide in a nice civilized place, like Coruscant or Kuat. As it happens, I actually speak all six dialects of Kuat, including the rare —"

"We're not going to Kuat," Luke said irritably. "And we're not *hiding*." He brushed a hand through his hair, already dusted with sand. Away from his home planet, he had forgotten the way the sand coated everything, inside and out. Luke squinted against the brutal twin suns and wiped the sweat off his forehead, smearing his face with sandy grit. Hard to believe he'd spent his whole life here. And yet, now that he was back, it was just as hard to believe he'd ever left. "We're here for Biggs."

True, no one in the Rebellion knew where they'd gone. And Leia was adamant that they not return to Yavin 4 until the Rebels had completed their investigation and discovered who wanted Luke dead. But Luke hadn't *run away* to Tatooine. He'd gotten a message the week before from his old friend Windy. The old gang was getting together, to mourn the death and celebrate the life of Biggs Darklighter. To remember the good old days.

The days before a TIE fighter blew Biggs out of the sky.

Luke had been there, seen it happen. One moment Biggs was there, the same confident flyboy he'd been back home, covering Luke as they attacked the Death Star.

Then, the next moment, nothing left but a cloud of debris, drifting into space.

Luke had promised Leia he wouldn't tell any of his old friends where he'd been these last few months, which meant he couldn't tell them of Biggs's last moments or his last act of heroism. But Luke was determined to give his old friend the sendoff he deserved.

He just had one stop to make first.

"This is where you lived?" Leia asked, trying to see past the ruined remnants of the moisture farm and imagine what the place must have looked like before it was destroyed. It would have been hard under any circumstances — the Empire had burned most of it, and looting Jawas had taken care of the rest. But it wasn't just that. Leia would never have admitted it, but to her, the whole planet looked like a pile of ruins. Broken buildings, broken people. She couldn't imagine anyone growing up here, much less Luke.

He nodded, pointing at the pile of crumbled pourstone. It was already half-covered by sand and Leia suspected that within a few years, the desert would have reclaimed all remnants of the Lars moisture farm. "My bedroom was over there," Luke said. "Some of the vaporators were spread out, all along there. They were always breaking down, but it's like Uncle Owen always says, 'You want to be a moisture farmer, you have to —'"

He snapped his mouth shut.

"What?" Leia asked, when he didn't continue.

Luke shook his head.

He didn't have to explain any further. Leia had her own memories, her own ruined past. Sometimes it was hard to remember that the people you'd lost were gone forever. Sometimes it was impossible to forget.

They stood quietly for several long moments, the wind spraying a fine mist of sand in their faces. Even the droids knew better than to speak.

"Do you want to get closer?" Leia finally asked. "See if . . . there's anything left to salvage?"

Luke hesitated for a moment, scanning the ruins, as if weighing the odds that anything could have survived the Imperial destruction. Then he gave himself a shake, and turned his back on his old home. Leia hurried after him as he headed toward the landspeeder. When she reached him, he offered her a smile — the first real smile she'd seen since they landed. "I think I have a better idea."

X-7 stood in the middle of Luke's quarters, an odd sensation churning in his gut: uncertainty.

He had volunteered his help with the investigation of the explosion. And, as an official part of that investigation, he'd ransacked Luke's room. He'd scavenged through piles of Luke's clothing; he'd torn apart Luke's mattress. Searched everywhere for some record, some clue to where Luke and Leia might have gone.

And he'd come up empty.

He'd begun slicing Luke's encrypted computer files, but it would take some time. Meanwhile, he'd find a way to search Leia's room next. This would be harder to do without raising suspicion, but he'd get it done. That wasn't his concern.

His concern was that he wouldn't find anything there, either.

His concern was that Luke had slipped through his fingers, and X-7 wouldn't be able to hunt him down.

X-7 wouldn't be able to complete the mission he'd been given by his master.

And that meant X-7 would be punished.

As he had been punished before.

"You've failed me," the Commander says.

X-7 squints into the blinding light. His master is a dark shadow, looming over him. X-7 is immobilized, pinned to the wall by durasteel binders. There is no escape from the Commander's wrath. But the binders are unnecessary. X-7 will bear his punishment. He belongs to the Commander. If the Commander wishes to destroy him, that is his right.

"The bounty hunter had been stalking the target for weeks," he reports. "He killed the target before I even arrived. There was nothing I could have done."

A sharp crack, as the Commander backhands him across the jaw. "No excuses!" he shouts. "You let someone else find the target first. You let someone kill him before he could be interrogated. There is no excuse for failure!"

But X-7 is explaining, not excusing. Only frightened men make excuses, and X-7 has no fear. The Commander took that from him, along with every other emotion, long ago. For X-7, there are only facts. Events. And results. Except that the only acceptable result is success.

And he has failed.

He waits for death.

"I've put too much time and money into training you," the Commander mutters. "But obviously it wasn't enough. Your training will continue."

X-7 knows what this means. Back in the dark cell that has been home for as long as he can remember. Back to the battles with carnivorous danchafs and ravenous reeks. Back to the neural shock treatments, frying his system again and again, until there was nothing left but the urge to follow orders. Back to the possibility of death lurking around every corner, behind every door.

"But first, you will be punished for your failure," the Commander says.

The Commander draws out his tools. The Neuronic whip. The Fire blade. The force pike. The nerve disrupter. And the Treppus-2 vibroblade.

A droid could have accomplished this task with ease, but the Commander prefers to administer punishments himself.

X-7 is unafraid. The Commander's displeasure worms inside of him, acid that eats him from within. His failure is a physical fact, a physical pain. There is nothing to life but pleasing the Commander; failing him is worse than death. Worse than anything imaginable. The Commander lifts the vibroblade. His favorite. X-7 closes his eyes, believing he has nothing more to fear.

He is wrong.

"*This* is your better idea?" Leia asked, stepping over a pile of womp rat dung as they wound their way through a desolate assemblage of decrepit pourstone dwellings. Luke had called Anchorhead a small settlement, but as far as Leia could tell, it was barely more than a power station and a couple of cantinas. All looked deserted.

"Come on!" Luke said happily, hurrying to the power station. "I bet the guys are already inside."

Leia looked dubiously at the low-slung building. The rickety walls and decaying roof seemed to be on the verge of collapse; anyone inside might well be risking their life. "You sure your friends will be *here*?" Leia asked, glancing at the heap of spare parts and prototype droids rusting by the door. On the other side of the entrance, a gaunt, sickly dewback tugged weakly at the fraying rope tying him to the tether post.

"Where else would they be?" Luke asked, grinning. "Aw, Tosche Station's great, you'll see."

There was a dull metallic roar as a massive sandcrawler rolled past the station. C-3PO cast a fearful look at the machine. R2-D2 issued an alarmed series of beeps.

"What are you two so worried about?" Luke asked. "It's just a bunch of Jawas."

"*Precisely* what I'm afraid of," C-3PO replied. "I knew coming to this planet was a bad idea. Why, we're surrounded by potential dangers! If we had only —"

"You know, there's a machine shop around back," Luke said quickly. "Why don't you and Artoo go see if they can buff up your platings and outfit you with some fresh recharge couplings?"

C-3PO straightened up. "Now that you mention it, it *has* been far too long since my last tune-up. And all this sand is *not* helping matters." He brushed an imaginary fleck of dust off his shoulder. "Did you hear that?"

C-3PO boasted to his counterpart as they hurried around the back. "Master Luke is always looking out for our best interests."

R2-D2 trilled and beeped.

"He is most certainly *not* trying to get rid of us!" C-3PO said indignantly.

Leia suppressed a smile. It dropped away as soon as she stepped into Tosche Station. The inside was even more cluttered and dirty than she would have expected. Dimly lit, with low ceilings and peeling walls, the station was packed full of overstuffed shelves and bins. Every spare surface was covered with grease and spare parts. There was a long counter toward the front, presumably for customers, when there were any. But the station was mostly empty, save for a few figures in the back, lounging around an old holopool table. They all looked up as the door opened.

"Skywalker!" one of them roared, jumping up from the table and throwing his arms around his old friend.

"Miss me, Windy?" Luke asked, grinning.

"Missed beating you at holopool," a burly young man said, chuckling as he drove a knuckle into Luke's shoulder. He dragged Luke over to the table, pounding him on the back. "Skywalker's back!" he announced. "All hail the conquering Wormie!" The group burst into a mocking cheer.

"You never mentioned your nickname was *Wormie*," Leia whispered, trying not to laugh.

Luke flushed red and shrugged. As he introduced her to his friends, Leia struggled to keep the jumble of names and faces straight. The burly man was Fixer, a mechanic who ran Tosche Station, when there was any business to do, which was rarely. Next came Camie, who was gazing at Fixer and tossing sweet dweezels into his gaping mouth. Windy and Deak, who Leia couldn't tell apart — but since they kept repeating each other, she supposed it didn't matter. And, silent in the corner, Jaxson, his flat head, squarish jaw, and dead stare giving him the look of a droid.

Leia noticed Luke give him an odd look, but Luke replaced it with a smile before anyone else could notice. "And this is Leia," Luke said, when the introductions were complete. "My, uh, copilot." They had agreed that no one needed to know that Leia was *Leia Organa*, Princess of Alderaan and founding member of the Rebel Alliance.

"So, tell us about it, Luke!" Windy urged him.

"About what?"

"Everything," Windy said. "What it's like up there!" He pointed to the ceiling.

"Same as down here," Jaxson said, scowling. "Whole galaxy's the same, from one end to the other."

"Like you'd know," Fixer teased. "You've never been farther from home than Mos Espa — and you only ended up there because you got lost on your way home from Beggar's Canyon."

Jaxson didn't laugh.

"I thought you were shipping out to the Academy," Luke said. "What happened?"

Jaxson shrugged. "Changed my mind. This is my home. Not ashamed of where I come from, unlike some people."

"Changed his tune, he means," Fixer said, still chuckling. "Right after he failed his entrance exams."

A sudden, awkward silence descended over the table, broken only by Camie's tinkling giggle.

Deak cleared his throat, looking uncomfortable. "So, tell us about it, Skywalker. What have you been doing all this time?"

"Yeah, Wormie, wow us," Jaxson added. "You find yourself a good job cleaning out the dianoga dung on a garbage scow?"

"More like smuggling spice through the Outer Rim and swindling Hutts from here to Barabi," Luke boasted.

Leia shot him a sharp glance. They'd agreed on a cover story — that Luke had found a job as a mechanic at a distant shipping outpost. What was Luke doing?

Fixer snorted. "Yeah, right, Wormie. And I'm an

Imperial admiral, shipping out next week to command my own Star Destroyer."

"It's true!" Luke said hotly. "You should see my ship. Fastest in the sector. We've done the Kessel Run in less than twelve — I mean, *eleven* parsecs!"

Leia tried not to roll her eyes. Boasts like this were one thing coming from a laserbrained spacer like Han — but coming from Luke, they sounded down-right ridiculous. His friends looked like they felt the same way.

All except Camie. "Really?" she asked, looking intrigued.

"How'd you get your hands on a ship?" Deak asked.

Jaxson rolled his eyes. "As if Skywalker could really go up against a Hutt," he scoffed. "Wormie probably hasn't even been offworld — he's probably been hiding out in Mos Espa, cleaning 'freshers."

"Not many 'fresher-cleaners with a hundred thousand credit bounty on their heads," Leia snapped.

Luke looked at her in surprise.

"Why don't you tell them about the time you rescued us from the Imperials on Bimmisaari, Luke," she suggested, giving Luke a quick wink. "Or how you nabbed that shipment of glitterstim from the gang of Rodians on Kubindi."

Windy and Deak's eyes widened in amazement. Camie turned the full blast of her adoring gaze onto

Luke. Even Fixer seemed impressed. "You really managed to score yourself a freighter?" he asked Luke. "Running with the spice smugglers and everything? How'd you manage that?"

Luke grinned — not his familiar earnest smile, but a cocky curl of the lips in perfect imitation of Han Solo. He lowered his voice. "Okay, boys, you want the real story? If you promise not to spread it around . . . ?"

They nodded eagerly, and Luke began spinning a tale Leia had heard many times from Han, about a death-defying run-in with some rival smugglers on the Bubble Cliffs of Nezmi. She smiled to herself. Luke's friends were looking at him like he was a hero. Sure, everything out of Luke's mouth was a lie, but the hero part was absolutely true.

"You stole a blaster shipment from the *Empire*?" Jaxson interrupted Luke angrily. "That's treason!"

"Aw, go crink yourself, Jaxson," Fixer said. "Like the kriffing Empire doesn't have enough blasters. Let him finish the story."

"Tell the truth, Luke," Windy said. "Did you steal those weapons for the Rebellion? You can tell us."

"Yeah, you can tell *us*," Deak seconded.

Luke offered them only a mysterious shrug. "Can't say who hired me for the job. Smuggler's code."

"Think the Alliance could use another smuggler?" Windy asked. "I'm not a bad pilot myself."

Deak shoved him. "Then how come you just crashed your third skyhopper this year?"

Jaxson smacked his hand down on the table. "You're all going to sit here and joke about joining up with that bunch of cowardly traitors?" he growled. "Today, of all days? We're here for Biggs, aren't we? He'd be ashamed of you all."

"Biggs gave his *life* for the Rebellion!" Luke blurted.

"Luke," Leia said quietly, hoping to remind him that he wasn't supposed to know how Biggs had died. He certainly couldn't admit to seeing it for himself. If anyone suspected Luke had been present for the Death Star explosion, he'd be in even more danger.

"Biggs was an officer in the Imperial Navy," Jaxson shot back. "He gave his life for the *Empire*, not your band of kriffing traitors."

"You don't know what you're talking about," Luke said, teeth gritted and face pale.

"If you're right," Jaxson said, "then he died a traitor. And the galaxy's better off without him." Camie gasped. Fixer glared, as Windy and Deak looked like they wanted to crawl under the table.

Luke balled his left hand into a fist. His right hand reached for his lightsaber. Leia grabbed his arm. "Luke, let it go," she urged him in a whisper.

He shook her off. "Say that again," he ordered Jaxson, in a low, dangerous voice. "I dare you."

CHAPTER FIVE

riggs Pe'et?" Han said, approaching a booth in the cantina's back corner inhabited by a grizzled Balosar. The creature wiggled its retractable antennapalps. Han had met a few Balosars in his day — it was a duplicitous, cowardly, greedy species, and he expected Griggs would be no exception. "Han Solo," he introduced himself, sliding into a seat. Chewbacca stayed on his feet, standing guard. "You said you wanted the best? You got him."

The Balosar had contacted the *Falcon* shortly after the ship jumped away from Yavin 4. He was looking for someone with "very particular skills" to acquire a "very particular package" — and he'd been told Han was the man to do it.

That was it. No details about the potential job or the potential fee. Just a name, Griggs Pe'et, and a time and location. Fourteen hundred hours, in a small gambling joint on Tythe, take it or leave it.

Han wasn't in the habit of taking jobs from just anyone.

Just anyone who could pay.

So he and Chewbacca had jumped to the Arkanis sector, and here he was. Ready for something new.

Kislov's Gambling Palace was a dead end club on a dead end planet, filled with dead-eyed spacers looking to make a quick buck. The room was claustrophobic and musty, the muttering quiet punctuated by the occasional shout of protest about a cheating sabacc dealer. (In Han's experience, *all* sabacc dealers cheated — it was your own fault if you played without knowing the rules of the game.) A dour Ychthytonian sloshed drinks behind the bar, juggling mugs of grog and caf in each of his four hands. The club looked like a gundark nest and smelled like wet bantha fur.

Han felt right at home.

"As we speak, an Imperial transport is ferrying a valuable shipment to the Imperial satellite station in the Zoma system," the Balosar said in a hushed tone.

"Shipment of what?" Han asked.

"That is not your concern yet," Griggs Pe'et said. "Your only concern is that *I* want the shipment — and I'm willing to pay for it."

"Oh yeah? How much?" Han asked.

"Ten thousand," Pe'et offered.

Han laughed. "You want me to infiltrate an Imperial station for ten thousand? You some kind of comedian?"

Chewbacca growled.

"Don't worry, buddy, I'm sure he was just kidding around," Han said. "No need to tear his arms off." He leaned toward the Balosar. "That's the thing about Wookiees. They can't take a joke. So how about we talk about the *real* price."

"What did you have in mind?" Pe'et hissed.

Han named a price that was double his usual — just enough to pay back Jabba, with a little leftover for a new exhaust port on the *Falcon*.

The alien's antennapalps began to vibrate, shuddering so hard Han half-expected his head to split in two. Pe'et frowned. "You drive a hard bargain, Solo. I could get ten men to do it for half that."

Han shrugged. "You want the best, you pay for the best." He jerked his head at Chewbacca, and they stood up together. "But if you'd rather find someone else —"

"Wait," the Balosar barked. "I'll pay. *When* I get the shipment."

"You'll pay half up front," Han said. "Or no deal."

Pe'et nodded. "Then we have an agreement?"

"We have an *offer*," Han said, enjoying himself. It felt good to be back in his element, doing what he did best. "My partner and I will have to discuss it."

The alien nodded again, then stared at them, as if waiting.

"*Alone,*" Han said.

Griggs Pe'et stood up, muttering something about why he hated dealing with humans. He tossed a data-card down on the table. "This will tell you how to reach me. I'll need a decision by tonight."

Once they were alone, Han kicked back in his chair, propping his legs on the table. "Looks like we got ourselves a job, buddy," he said contentedly.

Chewbacca barked a question.

"What's to discuss?" Han asked. "He's got credits, we've got a ship."

Chewbacca growled.

"All we *need* to know about him is that he's willing to pay us forty thousand," Han said.

Chewbacca growled again, and Han rolled his eyes.

"No, it's got nothing to do with the fact that it's an *Imperial* station," Han said. "I told you, I don't care what Leia and the rest of them think of me."

Chewbacca issued a low moan.

"Well of *course* we'll let them know if we find out something that can help," Han said irritably. "But that's not why I'm doing it. This is just a job, that's it."

"And Han Solo *never* lies down on the job," a familiar voice growled from behind him. "Ain't that right?"

Han reached for his weapon — then froze as he felt the cold muzzle of a blaster press against the back of his neck.

The Balosar crept into the dim alley behind the gambling club, his palm extended. The man in the tattered gray robe was waiting, his face still shrouded by a heavy hood.

"He says he needs to think it over," Griggs Pe'et said. "But if I know Solo, he'll take the job. You got my payment?"

The man slipped a credit chip out of his utility belt. "You'll find an additional ten thousand, to cover your silence," he said. "You'll get the rest when Captain Solo accepts the job. And, as agreed, if Solo is successful, you can keep the shipment."

The Balosar shoved the chip into a fold in his loose-fitting robe. "I still don't get it. You hire *me* to hire *Solo*, to steal a shipment that you don't even want? Doesn't make any sense."

"It doesn't have to make sense. Not to you," the man said. "You just have to give Solo the coordinates of the Imperial station and then forget you ever met me."

"Met who?" the Balosar asked, and slipped away into the darkness.

The man waited a moment, tipping his face up, as if breathing in the night. Only once he'd assured himself that he was truly alone, did he speak. "It is done."

CHAPTER SIX

Jaxson slammed his glass down on the table. He narrowed his eyes and leaned across the table toward Luke. "I *said*, the Rebellion is full of traitors," he repeated. "So if Biggs was a Rebel, then he was a traitor, too."

Luke stood up. "That's enough!"

"Oh yeah?" Jaxson asked, rising to his feet. He stood several centimeters taller than Luke, and his arms were broad and muscled from long days working on his family's moisture farm. "You gonna stop me, Wormie?"

"Maybe I am," Luke said, balling his fists.

"Guys, take it easy," Windy said.

"Luke, just let it go," Leia advised.

"Yeah, Luke," Jaxson simpered, in a parody of Leia's voice. "Be a good little boy and let it go."

Luke knew he should listen to Leia.

But.

Han wouldn't let it go, he thought to himself. And

after all, he'd told all his friends he was a pilot now, a smuggler, a tough and dangerous guy. Shouldn't he act the part?

Shouldn't he defend Biggs's honor, the only way a tough and dangerous smuggler would know how?

"Biggs was a hero," Luke said. And then he punched Jaxson in the stomach.

"Oooof!" Jaxson wheezed, doubling over. But in an instant, he was upright again, fists swinging wildly. He lunged at Luke. Windy jumped into the fight, trying to separate the two. Jaxson swung, Luke ducked, and Windy took the blow on his chin. He wheeled backward, slamming into Fixer, who toppled over in his chair.

"Watch it!" Fixer shouted, climbing to his feet and lashing out at Windy.

The station was still mostly empty, but there were a few stragglers loitering around the table who'd been waiting too long for a good fight. In Anchorhead, not much else ever broke the monotony of the day. Soon they were all on their feet, cheering and stomping and throwing punches and kicks at random.

A slim, rat-faced Ranat went sailing through the air and crashed through a window, spraying the station with a shower of transparisteel. There were a few cries of "traitor!" and "Imperial slime!" but it was obvious that most people didn't know what the fight was about nor did they care. Tosche Station was filling up, as passersby heard the commotion and hurried in to join the fun. A stocky, muscled woman slung a punch at a bedraggled Ryn, who broke a chair over the head of a scruffy human with a patch across his left eye. Leia pressed herself into a corner, rolling her eyes at a trio of Dugs, who were taking turns stomping on each others' heads.

But in the center of the chaos, Luke hadn't forgotten what was at stake. Jaxson wrapped an arm around his neck and twisted him into a choke hold. Luke gasped for breath. "This is what we do to traitors!" Jaxson growled.

Luke stomped down hard on Jaxson's instep, then dug an elbow sharply into his stomach. Jaxson flinched and his grip loosened, only for a moment, enough time for Luke to wriggle out of his grasp. Jaxson swung his fists, but Luke darted out of the way, and none of the blows landed. Luke ducked behind Jaxson and wrapped his arms around the larger man's waist, twisting him off balance and kicking his legs out from under him. Jaxson toppled to the ground with a thump and clatter. With a roar, he snatched Luke's ankle and yanked with all his strength. Luke went flying.

The thunderous crack of laserfire hitting the ceiling made everyone pause and look up. A large man emerged from the back room, hoisting a blaster. The first shot had gone straight up. But now he had the muzzle aimed out at the crowd. Merl Tosche spent as little time at the power station as he could afford to do. But when he was at work, he hated to be disturbed. "Enough!" he roared.

With a shrug and a grin, the fighters dusted themselves off, shook hands, and slunk out of the station. That was the thing about most fights on Tatooine — it didn't take much to get them started, but it took even less to end them.

Most, but not all. Luke wasn't ready to give up. Neither was Jaxson.

Windy grabbed Luke by the shoulders and pulled him to his feet. Jaxson lunged forward, but Deak grabbed his shirt and dragged him backward. The two glared at each other.

"You children done playing?" Leia asked dryly, gazing at the debris strewn across the station. A rickety JR-8 maintenance droid was already sweeping away the worst of it, sucking shattered fuel cells and puddles of spilled ruby bliel into its hollow durasteel belly.

"This isn't a game," Luke said.

"No, it's not," Jaxson agreed.

Windy forced a grin and slapped Luke awkwardly on the back. "Let's forget the whole thing," he suggested. "Empire, Rebellion, who cares? What's that got to do with us?"

"Yeah," Fixer agreed. "Whoever's running the galaxy, the suns will keep rising and the vaporators will keep sucking moisture. Vader can't bring water to the desert, any more than the Rebels can tame a krayt dragon. Tatooine will always be Tatooine."

"Fixer's right," Camie said, slipping her arms around her fiancé and nestling her head on his shoulder. "It's not our problem."

Luke shook his head. "You don't understand. If you knew what was really going on out there —"

"Like *you* know?" Jaxson scoffed. "You think you're so much smarter than us because you left and we stayed? You walk away from your responsibilities to run around the galaxy playing space pilot, and you want to come back here and tell us *we* don't understand?"

"That's not what I meant," Luke protested.

"You think you're so special, just because you can pilot a ship," Jaxson jeered. "But I'm a better pilot than you any day."

Luke scowled. "I've seen you fly," he retorted. "You couldn't drive a skyhopper twenty meters without crashing into a dune."

"Oh yeah?"

"Yeah!"

"You think you're so much better? How about you prove it!" Jaxson challenged.

"Anytime, any place," Luke said.

"Tomorrow. Race in Beggar's Canyon. We'll thread the Needle. At least, *one* of us will."

Luke hesitated.

"Scared?" Jaxson jeered.

"Scared for *you*, maybe." Only two people had ever successfully threaded the Needle. Luke was one of them; Jaxson wasn't the other.

"Jaxson, don't be crazy!" Camie squealed.

"Yeah, you got nothing to prove," Windy added. He'd been in the cockpit the first time Luke had threaded the Needle, and he still looked traumatized by the memory.

Jaxson ignored them, keeping his eyes fixed on Luke. "You in?"

"Tomorrow at sunset," Luke said. "If you're crazy enough to go through with it." He stalked out of the station without waiting for a response. A moment later, Leia came up behind him and gently rested a hand on his shoulder. He shrugged her off.

"I'm fine," he said, and turned around. There was nothing gentle in her expression.

"I wasn't going to ask if you were *fine*," she snapped. "I was going to ask if you were *crazy*. We came here to keep you safe, and what's the first thing you do? Start a stupid fight over nothing!"

"It's not nothing," Luke protested. "You heard him."

Leia shook her head in disgust. "I thought you knew better than that," she chided him. "You were acting like a child in there. No, worse, you were acting like *Han*."

Luke brightened. "You think so?"

"That's *not* a compliment." Leia rubbed her hands across her eyes in exhaustion. "This isn't like you."

"Maybe that's the point," Luke said. "*Han* never runs away from danger. But here I am, hiding out here like a scared profrogg."

"*Han* ran away from *us!*" Leia pointed out. "Or are you forgetting?"

"He had his reasons," Luke said, wishing he knew what they were. "And that's not the point. The point is, I'm not running away again. Especially not from the Needle. That doesn't scare me."

"Why do I get the feeling that it should?" Leia asked. "What is it?"

Luke told her about the canyon, a long, jagged gash in the desert that had once been a part of the old Boonta Eve Classic Podrace circuit. With its alarmingly sharp twists and turns, it made the perfect training ground for aspiring pilots. Luke had spent plenty of hours out there, practicing his maneuvers and using womp rats for target practice.

Then there was the Needle.

"The Stone Needle's nearly twenty meters high," Luke explained, "and most racers go around it. But if you can manage to slip through the eye of the Needle, you can shave four, maybe five seconds off your time."

Not to mention, prove that you were the boldest and best pilot around.

"So why doesn't everyone go through the Needle?" Leia asked, like she already knew the answer.

"Well . . . lots of people *try*," Luke admitted. "But it's risky. If you're off by even a meter . . ."

As he spoke, Leia's lips pressed tighter and tighter together. Her cheeks blazed red.

"No," she said, shaking her head. "*No.* That's too risky."

"Aw, it's no risk for me," Luke said. "I've done it before. It's a piece of pika cake. After what I've done? The Podrace on Muunilinst? The Death —"

Leia silenced him with a look, and cast a meaningful glance over her shoulder. Luke tensed, as the hairs on the back of his neck stood to attention. He was suddenly convinced that someone was watching them. But the streets of Anchorhead were deserted.

"Anyway, that was different," Leia said impatiently. "You were risking your life for something important. Not to show off."

"*This* is important," Luke insisted. "It's not about whether I'm a better pilot. It's not even about me. You know who was the first person to ever thread the Needle? Biggs. This is for *him*. Maybe I can't tell anyone how he died — I can't prove that he died a hero. But I can do this. I can do this for him."

"This Jaxson guy . . . ." Leia shook her head. "That's some friend you've got there."

Luke bristled. "He's not *my* friend. We never used to hang around with him, but . . . I guess a lot's changed since I left."

"Not that much," Leia said, offering a half smile. "He's still not your friend."

Luke laughed hesitantly, not sure if that meant she wasn't angry anymore.

"You're telling me that you really believe if you beat Jaxson in a skyhopper race, you'll be proving that Biggs is a hero?" she asked, dead serious again.

Luke nodded.

"And that if you don't race, or if you lose, it will mean to all of your friends that Jaxson's right about the Alliance and about Biggs?"

Luke nodded again.

"You do realize that makes no sense, right?" she asked.

"Not to you, maybe," Luke said quietly.

"But it does to you?"

Luke nodded a third time, and when he raised his head, he held her gaze steadily.

Leia breathed out a sigh, then grinned. "In that case . . . I guess you'd better win."

Far across the Western Dune Sea stood a fortress, whose population of guards, chefs, dancers, thieves, and slaves was several times that of Anchorhead. In the bowels of the palace, spider-like creatures skittered through the murky depths, each one's mechanical arms powered by a brain in a jar. These were all that remained of the B'omarr monks, who had erected the great fortress centuries before. Now they clung to the shadows, while another usurped the seat of their power.

The usurper required a very large seat.

"Who's next?" Jabba the Hutt roared in Huttese from his massive throne. The groveling courtiers who packed his throne room shrank away from the slug's booming voice. He slapped his tail impatiently against the dais, so hard that the floor beneath him vibrated. Jabba was the sector's biggest crime lord, the shadowy force behind every dirty deal in the sector. His power was such that with a word, he could bring down governments, torpedo corporations, and, if he chose to do so, perhaps destroy a small city.

But the obese Hutt's favorite games were those he could play from home; his favorite toys were the ones who cowered before his throne, begging for mercy. Too stupid to know it would never be granted.

A thin, stooped human shivered under his glare. Jabba smiled, his mouth widening enough so that he could have swallowed up the man whole. He was always glad to see a human; they tended to be the stupidest of all. And the most fun.

A thick scar crawled from beneath the collar of the human's ragged brown tunic. It traversed the length of his neck and split his weathered face down the middle.

"You dare interrupt my dessert?" Jabba asked. One of Jabba's servants dangled a wriggling gorg over the Hutt's open mouth. Jabba's massive tongue tickled the gorg. At Jabba's command, the servant let the creature drop. It disappeared, squealing and keening, into Jabba's gaping maw. He swallowed it with a loud gulp. "Speak!" he commanded.

The human mumbled something, but his words were drowned out by the chattering and chuckling of Jabba's court.

"Louder!" Jabba said. "Rancor got your tongue? Because that can be arranged. HO! HO! HO!" There was a brief pause, and then the room burst into laughter. Jabba raised his twig-like arm, and the sound stopped abruptly.

"Honorable Jabba," the man muttered in Huttese, only a bit louder than the first time. "Thank you for this audience. I've come to report that Luke Skywalker has returned to Tatooine. He's in Anchorhead!"

"*Who?* What do I care about Luke Skyhopper?" Jabba roared. "Seize him," he ordered his Gamorrean guards. "The rancor needs his supper."

"Wait!" the man cried, as a phalanx of brutish Gamorreans closed in on him, their green snouts snuffling eagerly at the thought of another kill. "Luke Skywalker is a known associate of Han Solo!"

A murmur rippled through the room. Jabba's hatred of Solo was well known. The pilot had crossed him one too many times, and Jabba had offered a reward for any information leading to his capture.

"Solo?" Jabba hissed, gobbling down another gorg. He turned to Bib Fortuna, his trusted second in command. "Is this true?"

The Twi'lek nodded, his long, fleshy tentacles swirling around his neck. "We've received reports that the two are close. Skywalker's been traveling with the *Millennium Falcon*. If he's on Tatooine . . ."

"Then Solo must be close," Jabba said, gurgling with pleasure. Soon Han Solo's body would be hanging on

Jabba's wall, a reminder to all of what happened when you betrayed the ruler of the Hutts. "This Skycrabber will lead us to Solo." They would snatch the human, use him as bait. Solo would come running.

And if he didn't . . . well, you could never have enough slaves.

All Jabba needed was the right bounty hunter for the job. He snatched a Klatooine paddy frog from the tank at his feet, crushing it into a pulp and stuffing it into his maw. As the salty reptile juice ran down his bloated face, he realized he had just the creature for the job. "Get me Bossk," he commanded. And at his word, two of the Gamorreans went running. The Trandoshan bounty hunter would show his scaly face by nightfall. Or suffer the consequences.

"Still here?" Jabba shouted at the human cowering before him.

Shaking, the man mumbled something under his breath.

Bib Fortuna leaned toward Jabba. "The human wants his reward," he hissed.

"Reward?" Jabba asked loudly. "*Reward?* HO HO! This human wants a reward!" Again, the room laughed with Jabba. And kept laughing as Jabba pressed a button on the end of his long hookah pipe.

The human cowered, squeezing his eyes shut, and the laughing grew even louder. But he wasn't in pain . . .

yet. Still shaking, he opened his eyes to see a small pile of credits in front of him.

"Thank you, Honorable Jabba," the man murmured, bowing low and piling the credits into his threadbare tunic, "you truly are the greatest of the Hutts." He kept bowing as he scuttled out of the room, a few credits scattering in his wake.

As the laughter swelled, the band struck up another tune, filling the room with jaunty music. Jabba snapped his fingers for another gorg, when Bib Fortuna leaned and whispered into his ear.

"Another one?" Jabba asked. "Make him wait."

Bib Fortuna hesitated. "But this one, he has . . . debts."

Jabba smiled. "Very well. Send him in."

A Toydarian buzzed into the room, flitting nervously and looking over his shoulder, taking in the courtiers and henchmen.

Jabba began to shake with laughter. "Block the exits! I will now have my justice."

CHAPTER EIGHT

It wasn't the first time Han had felt the cold durasteel of a blaster muzzle against his skin. When it came to life and death situations, he was an old pro.

Still, all things considered, he'd rather be playing a hand of sabacc.

"Hands in the air, and turn around," the voice said. "*Slowly.*"

Han raised his hands and turned. *Slowly.*

The blaster was a Merr-Sonn J-1 Happy Surprise hold-out model, small enough to fit in the palm of a hand, useless at distances of more than three meters. Deadly at point-blank range. A pale, stubby finger was itching to pull the trigger. And attached to it, the hand, the arm, the shoulder, the face of a man Han hadn't seen in years. A man whose last words to Han had been, "Next time I see you, you're dead."

Han grinned.

Chewbacca roared in frustration, knowing that the wrong move could get Han killed.

"Would you shut that Wookiee up!" the man yelled, pressing the blaster to Han's forehead. A few of the other gamblers looked over, then shrugged and turned back to their gaming tables. In a place like this, you didn't pay too much attention to what anyone else was doing. Not if you wanted to walk out in one piece.

"Easy, Chewie," Han said, hoping that the Wookiee wouldn't do anything rash. "Lore here isn't going to shoot me, are you, Lore?"

Chewbacca barked a question.

"Yeah, Lore and I go *way* back," Han said, winking at his assailant. "Long time no see, Lore. How's it going?"

"Better, now." Avik Lore — failed musician, failed gambler, failed cantina owner, successful smuggler — snarled at Han.

"Don't tell me you're still mad about that little incident back on Dubrillon," Han said wearily.

Lore's eyes widened. "*Incident?* You shot me!"

Han shrugged. "Not on purpose," he pointed out. "Besides, it was just a flesh wound. Don't be such a baby."

"I couldn't sit down for a month!"

Chewbacca let loose a hiccupy gurgle that Han knew was suppressed Wookiee laughter. Lore shot him a sharp glance. Chewbacca pounded his chest in a good imitation of a Wookiee not at all amused.

"How was I supposed to know it was you behind that door?" Han wheedled. "I though it was the G'looth Brothers!"

"You could have *asked*," Lore said. "You could have knocked. Or you could have opened the door and taken a peek before you let loose with your blaster. You could have done a million things."

"Could have," Han said. "Didn't."

Lore sighed. "I know, I know, rule number one —"

"Always shoot first," Han finished with him. "And I always do. Best way to keep breathing."

"Not when you're the one who gets shot," Lore growled.

Han was getting tired of staring down the barrel of a blaster just because Lore was a little grouchy about some flesh wound from a hundred years ago. Slowly, Lore's blaster tracing his every move, Han rose to his feet. "Look, friend, fun as this little reunion has been —"

"Who said you could stand up?"

"Well now, I don't know," Han mused, raising his left hand as if to scratch his chin in thought. "Who said that?" Ever so slowly, he let his fingers creep toward his forehead, toward the muzzle of the blaster, until —

"Hey!" Lore shouted, as Han wrapped a hand around the muzzle. "You think I won't shoot you?"

"No . . ." While Lore was distracted by the tussle over his weapon, Han's right hand darted to his holster and whipped out his DL-44 heavy blaster, optimized for quick draw capabilities. "Not if I fire first," he said, grinning, his blaster held steady, inches from Lore's face.

Lore's blaster didn't wobble.

"You think you're faster on the trigger than me?" Lore challenged.

Han grinned. "Either I can prove it to you, or you can lower your blaster, and I'll lower my blaster, and you can buy me a bottle of lum."

Lore squinted, knitting his eyebrows together like two wriggling hagworms. "*You're* buying," he said finally.

"Done," Han said. "On three?"

They counted down together.

"One . . ."

"Two . . ."

"Three —" On three, each man blasted a hole in the wall, just behind the other's head.

"Just a warning," they said, in sync, then burst into laughter.

Han slapped his old friend on the back. "Always good to see you, Lore. So how about that lum you're buying me?"

"*You're* buying," Lore said, sliding comfortably into

a seat next to Chewbacca. The Wookiee glared suspiciously and grumbled under his breath.

"Don't mind Chewie," Han said, waving over a serving droid and ordering a round of drinks and a bowl of won-wons for the Wookiee. "He doesn't like it when people try to shoot me."

"I know how he feels," Lore said ruefully, rubbing the site of his old blaster wound.

Chewbacca took a large gulp of won-wons and growled.

"Long before your time," Han replied. "Lore and I met when I saved him from an angry nexu."

"He was only angry because you blew up his cave!" Lore reminded Han, launching into the story of the carnivorous beast.

Han laughed as the memories came flooding back. It felt good to talk about old times, times before he'd met Luke or Leia, before he'd gotten all tangled up with the Rebel Alliance. Back then his only worry had been when the next job would come in, and his only cause had been himself.

"Hey, Lore, you got anything going on?" he asked suddenly, the beginnings of an idea taking shape.

"Got a routine run to Siskeen for a shipment of rock wart eggs," Lore said. "Could do it in my sleep."

"What if I had something more . . . interesting?"

Han asked, leaning forward and lowering his voice. Chewbacca issued a warning growl, but Han ignored him. Sure, Lore was a little rough around the edges, but that was part of his charm. "I've got a job coming up," Han confided, "a big one. And I could use a little of your brand of help."

Chewbacca growled louder.

"Lore knows this sector like the back of his hand," Han pointed out. "And I know he's not afraid to tangle with some Imperials — not if the price is right."

Lore's ears perked up. "And the price would be?"

"Twenty thousand," Han lied. "Split down the middle, seventy-thirty."

"Last I checked, the middle's a little closer to fifty," Lore said.

Han grinned. "My job — my math."

"Sixty-forty," Lore proposed. "And I might just know where you can get some Imperial docking codes. You're pulling one on the Empire, that could come in handy."

Han glanced at Chewbacca. "What do you think, buddy?"

Chewbacca made it clear he didn't think much of it — not the idea, not Avik Lore. But he'd come around. Han grasped Lore's hand, and they shook on it. "Just like the good old days," he said happily.

Lore winced and, once again, brushed his fingers against his old blaster scars. "Let's hope not."

The man in the gray, hooded robe slipped out of the gambling club, satisfied. Han Solo would take the job. He would infiltrate the Imperial satellite station, and while there, he would find . . .

Well, that was the question, wasn't it?

The man returned to the alley behind the club. These days, he felt more comfortable in the shadows. "I still don't like this," he said, to the open air.

He paused for a moment, feeling rather silly, waiting for a response that might never come.

"We agreed on this course." The figure shimmering before him was solid and not solid, there and not there, all at the same time. He glowed with an inner light, and yet the night remained dark. "Search yourself, Ferus. You know this is right."

"Perhaps. But it feels wrong." Ferus Olin was decades away from his apprenticeship at the Jedi Temple, a sanctuary that no longer existed. And yet, even from beyond the grave, Master Obi-Wan Kenobi still had the ability to make him feel like a rebellious Padawan. Not that Ferus had ever *been* a rebellious Padawan. He'd done everything he was told, accepted every order without question, performed every task perfectly and without hesitation — until the day he'd made a fateful mistake, and someone had been killed. Not just someone. A friend.

And not just my mistake, he thought. *Anakin's, too.*

Ferus had walked away from the Jedi Order. Forever, he thought. And yet here he was, decades later, learning at the feet of a Master all over again.

He had gotten a valuable lesson all those years ago, the day Thel-Tanis had died. Sometimes a wrong decision can get someone killed. Ferus had vowed never to make such a decision again.

Yet he'd made several.

"Whatever information is on that station, I can get it myself," he said. "There's no reason to risk Han's life."

"The life is his to risk," Obi-Wan said. "The decision his to make."

"But we're not *giving* him a decision!" Ferus countered. "We're manipulating him."

After nearly two decades undercover on Alderaan, looking out for Princess Leia's safety, Ferus had struck out on his own. Darth Vader was on the trail of the pilot who had blown up the Death Star, and he couldn't be allowed to discover the truth. If he found Luke — if he guessed the truth — all would be lost.

Ferus was on the trail of First Lieutenant Slej Hant, an Imperial officer whom Vader had assigned to ferret out the information. But as he passed through the

Arkanis sector, one of Ferus's informants had tipped him off about another Imperial on the same mission. According to the informant, a high-ranking officer had parked himself on a satellite station in the Zoma system, a nearly forgotten outpost that would keep him far from Vader's prying eye. Ferus's spy claimed that the man was desperate to find the Death Star's destroyer before Vader did . . . and he was getting close.

But so was Slej Hant, and he was about to take off for the Subterrel sector, a far-flung corner of space beyond the Outer Rim. An Imperial agent could have no possible business there.

Unless he was headed for Polis Massa, the arid, remote planetoid where Luke Skywalker and Leia Organa had been born.

Ferus was torn. Worried as he was about this other Imperial, he couldn't allow Vader's minion to ferret out Luke and Leia's identities. Obi-Wan, as usual, had cut through the confusion, speaking with infuriating certainty, even from beyond the grave. "Han Solo will infiltrate the station. He'll find the answers that he needs."

"Solo?" Ferus had asked in confusion. "The pilot?" They'd met briefly on Delaya, but Ferus had paid little attention. Because Delaya had also been the site of his first meeting with Luke Skywalker. Every moment they had spent together, Ferus had been wracked with doubts.

Should he tell the boy the truth? Or accede to Obi-Wan's wishes, and let him chart his own course for just a little longer?

Amidst all the confusion, Han Solo had barely made an impression.

"The pilot." Obi-Wan's cryptic smile was just as infuriating in death as in life. "He's on his own now, searching. He needs direction. And he will find it on the Zoma station."

"That makes no sense," Ferus had complained. Yet he had done as Obi-Wan requested, opening himself up to the Force. Drawing in its strength and its wisdom as he groped for the way to move forward. And he felt it too. Obi-Wan was right.

This was Han's mission. He would infiltrate the satellite station in the Zoma system and find the answers they all needed to save Luke and Leia.

If he survived.

Luke hunched over the controls of his T-16 skyhopper, waiting for Fixer to set off the starter flare. He missed the familiar feel of his old skyhopper, which was long gone, destroyed along with the rest of the Lars moisture farm. But this one, which he'd borrowed from Windy, would get the job done.

Luke engaged the repulsorlifts, hovering a few meters above the ground. He gave the thrusters a gentle push, tipping the T-16 slightly to its side and then upright again, just to get a feel for it. It had been a long time since he'd flown one of these. The last time he'd raced, he'd been curled into the cramped seat of a Podracer, a rickety bucket tethered to roaring engines that, without warning, could flip you up and out. Compared to that, the skyhopper was like a kiddie ride. Its central airfoil offered significant stability, and its gyrostabilizers would allow Luke to make hairpin turns and wild spins without fear of spiraling out of control.

No, winning a skyhopper race wasn't a matter of balance. It was a matter of speed — whether you could push the ion engine past its 1,200 kilometer an hour capacity. It was a matter of agility — whether you could gauge the angles and hit your marks better than your competition.

And, when it came to the Stone Needle, it was a matter of daring — whether you were willing to risk your life, just to win a race.

"Ready!" Fixer called, raising the signal flare over his head. "Set!"

Luke glanced at Jaxson out of the corner of his eye, then turned back to his own controls, letting the rest of the world fall away as he focused on the course ahead of him.

For you, Biggs, he thought, ready to push the thrusters to their limits.

He would risk anything to win this race.

Fixer squeezed the trigger, and the sky flashed red with the signal blast. *"Go!"*

Luke took off at the signal, his skyhopper shooting forward a split second before Jaxson's. Desert streamed past, blurring into a mud of browns and grays. The small craft hummed beneath him, responding smoothly to his every shift and turn.

The walls of Beggar's Canyon rose steeply on either side, hundreds of meters of solid sandstone that would crush him in an instant if he veered off course. Luke didn't think about the risks. He focused on the jagged trail, the thunder of the engine, and the purpling sky overhead. He didn't dare look back at Jaxson's skyhopper, but he knew if he did, he'd see a cloud of dust spattering the transparisteel of Jaxson's cockpit window. As the kilometers flew past, Luke stayed ahead, and he intended to keep it that way.

He spotted a womp rat, just a blur, streaking past beneath him, and almost smiled, remembering the days when he, Windy, and Biggs could waste a whole afternoon chasing the scraggly creatures through the canyon. During those years, all he'd wanted was to get away — from his aunt and uncle's moisture farm, from Tatooine, from his life. Now he couldn't remember what he'd been running from.

But maybe life was like a skyhopper race: you couldn't look back.

Luke forced his mind back to the track. He rocketed through the straightaway, then whipped the T-16 sharply to the right, making it around Dead Man's Turn with only centimeters to spare between him and the canyon wall. Behind him, he heard the scream of durasteel on rock, as Jaxson's skyhopper gouged out a piece of the canyon while rounding the curve. It bought Luke a few precious seconds, and he pulled even farther ahead, reaching the Stone Needle while Jaxson was still navigating the Sandy Jaws. Luke sucked in his breath. His hands tightened on the controls. The spire stretched nearly twenty meters from the canyon floor — but from this distance, the eye of the Needle appeared only a few meters across, no wider than the skyhopper itself. Luke knew from experience that it *was* wider — but only just.

He was far enough ahead that he could win the race without threading the Needle. But that would be a coward's victory.

Don't let 'em see you sweat, kid, he heard Han's voice in his head, and found himself wishing that the cocky pilot was by his side.

Of course, if he were here, he'd never let me *have the controls*, Luke thought with a grin.

"You want to back out, now's the time." Jaxson's taunt came through the comlink loud and clear.

Luke didn't bother to respond. He just pushed the throttle, speeding toward the Needle. It was all about precision. Lining up the ship with the narrow opening. Coming in at exactly the right angle, at exactly the right speed. No room for error. Error meant smashing into the tower of rock at 1,200 kilometers an hour.

Focus.

Forget about Jaxson, about the navigational computer, about the risk of crash, the risk of death. Let the ship become an extension of himself. Let its wings become his wings, its gyrostabilizers as much a part of him as his arms and legs. Luke let the rest of the world fade away, until there were only two things left in his galaxy. The ship and the Needle.

Just a little faster, just a little farther, and —

"Blast it!" Luke shouted, as his instrument screens blazed red with alerts. Navigation failure, steering failure, engine failure . . . every system was going wonky. It had to be a false alarm, except — *"Blast!"* Luke cried again, as the ship bucked and shuddered beneath him. He veered sharply to the right, away from the Needle, just before its rocky jaws snapped off his central airfoil.

"Mayday!" Jaxson cried through the comlink, as his skyhopper made an erratic loop around the rocky spire. "Something's wrong with the ship, I think it's —" The comlink went dead, and out of the corner of his eye, Luke saw Jaxson's skyhopper make a steep dive, dropping toward the ground at a sharp angle and an alarming speed.

And then Luke's engine cut out. The skyhopper plunged downward. Luke pulled back hard, trying to catch an updraft. If he could glide for just a few more kilometers, he could come in shallowly enough to crash-land. Rather than just crash. But the steering wouldn't respond. The alarms buzzed and blared as the skyhopper dropped out of the sky. Luke struggled to hold it horizontal.

This is it, he thought, as the ground rose up quickly. Time seemed to slow down, as it had back on Yavin 4, before the speeder exploded. But this time, it didn't matter. Luke couldn't just jump out; he'd modified his old T-16 for ejection capabilities, but that skyhopper was long gone. He had no choice but to go down with the ship.

The seconds dripped by, slow as melting dweezel taffy, and Luke had just enough time to admire the way the suns lit up the Stone Needle, lending the thin tower of rock a golden glow. *It looks like a lightsaber,* Luke marveled, wondering what would happen to his own, if he didn't make it.

And then the ground finally arrived, with a long scream of durasteel on desert rock.

Time's up.

There were only two pairs of electrobinoculars, so Leia had to share hers with Camie and Fixer. That was fine. She didn't have much interest in watching the race, and she certainly didn't need to see Luke thread the Needle. She'd seen him pull off more impressive stunts than that.

And more dangerous ones, she reminded herself, trying not to worry. She was furious at Luke for risking his life on something so stupid. After they'd come all this way to protect him. She wasn't about to encourage his foolishness by cheering him on.

But she was still curious. And every once in a while she grabbed a turn at the electrobinocs.

So she was the one peering through the lenses when Jaxson's ship dropped out of the sky, and a moment later, Luke's followed. There one minute, gone the next.

She was the one scanning the horizon for some sign of them, some movement.

She was the one who saw the ground spit up a cloud of fire.

But everyone saw the sky flare an angry red. And everyone saw the smoke.

Camie gasped. Someone put a hand on Leia's shoulder. She shook it off.

"He's fine," she said, aware that she sounded like a droid, flat and empty.

Fixer had grabbed the electrobinoculars and was peering intently at the crash site. "We've got to get out there," he said. "If they're going to have any chance at all —"

"He's *fine*," Leia insisted again.

She felt numb.

Numbly, she piled into a rusted landspeeder with Windy, Deak, and the droids. Luke's droids. Fixer and

Camie rode behind them. Numbly, she took the controls and steered toward the smoke. And numbly, she finally arrived at the crash site.

Two sites, really. Two scarred holes in the ground, strewn with smoldering wreckage. Twisted pieces of durasteel, broken shards of transparisteel. Smoke and fire. But no Jaxson. No Luke.

"Their bodies —" Fixer choked on the word. "A fire like that, it could have burned 'em up." Windy and Deak were identically pale, identically slack-jawed.

Leia shook her head and wiped a bead of sweat from her cheek. She gazed out at the desert. The sunburnt landscape was motionless. Nothing but kilometers of empty sand. *Where are you, Luke?* she thought. *Where did you go?*

"He's out there somewhere," she said.

"Where would they go?" Fixer asked skeptically. "And after a crash like that, how could they —"

He didn't finish the thought. He didn't have to. Leia understood: *You saw the crash. You saw the explosion. How could they be in any shape to walk away?*

"He's fine," she said. "If . . . if he wasn't, I would know."

"How?" Fixer challenged.

I don't know, she thought. But she allowed herself no doubts. Luke was alive. Somehow.

Somewhere.

CHAPTER TEN

Luke opened his eyes, squinting against the bright sun. He was lying on his side, his right cheek planted against the ground. The arid, empty landscape stretched to the horizon. The Stone Needle was nowhere to be seen. Nor was his skyhopper. There was nothing in sight but sand.

He remembered the crash.

Uncle Owen's going to kill me! he thought ruefully.

And then he remembered everything else.

This is not a good time for me to piloting anything.

Luke tried to sit up, but something was stopping him. Binders, around his wrists, around his ankles. And around his chest and knees, thick cords binding him to another person. Luke craned his neck around as far as it would go.

"Jaxson!" he hissed. "Jaxson!" Louder this time. But the body attached to him didn't move.

Something else did.

"Awake already?" snarled the massive green creature hulking over him. Luke recognized the distinctive scaled face, clawed hands, and razor sharp jaws of a Trandoshan, a race of aggressive reptilian warriors. This one was taller than average, his scaly limbs bursting from a bright orange flight suit that had clearly been designed for a creature much smaller than him. Luke wondered what had happened to the suit's original owner. He suspected that the blast rifle slung around the Trandoshan's neck might have had something to do with it. The Trandoshan flicked his long tongue at Luke. "You've got a pretty hard head. For a human."

Luke struggled to move, but Jaxson's immobile body held him in place.

"You did something to our skyhoppers," Luke accused the Trandoshan.

Bossk widened his jaws in a smile. "The pulse generator wiped out every electrical system in a forty kilometer radius. Namely: yours."

"Why?" Luke said. "We're not your enemy. I don't even know who you are!"

"But *I* know who *you* are," the Trandoshan said. "Luke Skywalker. Friend to that galactic scourge Han Solo. And *he's* got plenty of enemies." The Trandoshan straightened up, smoothing out his flight suit. "I'm surprised none of them came to me sooner. You want a job done right, Bossk is the one to do it."

He was a bounty hunter, Luke realized. Which meant there was no point in trying to talk him out of it. Hunters were notoriously merciless and single-minded when it came to pursuing their bounty. But there was no reason Jaxson had to pay.

If he could only reach his lightsaber . . .

That was a useless wish. The Trandoshan, perhaps not realizing it was a weapon, had left the lightsaber where it was, hanging from a low belt around Luke's hips. But his hands and arms were bound tightly behind his back. Much as he strained, the lightsaber was out of reach.

"Who hired you?" Luke asked, hoping to learn something that would help him.

The Trandoshan offered only an icy smile. "You'll find out soon enough. Though you'll wish you hadn't."

"At least let my friend go," Luke said. "He's got nothing to do with this. He's never even met Han."

"This worm?" Bossk asked. "Head softer than yours, it seems. He might already be dead. And if he's not, he will be soon."

"He's done nothing!"

"The Scorekeeper rewards triumph, not mercy," Bossk said. "You expect me to sacrifice my jagganath points for your soft-headed *human*?"

Luke groaned. He'd heard all about the Trandoshans from Han, who bore a heavy grudge against the race of notorious Wookiee-hunters. Trandoshans believed they would be greeted after their death by an all-powerful Scorekeeper who would tally up the number of points they'd achieved and offer them a divine reward.

They accrued points by killing.

"Our friends will come after us," Luke threatened him.

Bossk's lips widened, revealing his jagged teeth. He spit out a harsh, rasping noise, his tongue flickering. The laugh of a lizard. "Your friends think you're dead," he said. "A few fragmentation grenades saw to that."

"They'll come for me," Luke said steadily.

Bossk shrugged. "Night's coming," he said. "That'll make a nice dream." Then, without warning, his clawed foot shot out and caught Luke in the stomach, hard enough to send him and Jaxson rolling a few meters through the sand.

As the twin suns dipped beneath the horizon, Bossk dragged Luke and Jaxson into a shallow cave, then lay down across its entrance. Luke realized even the burly Trandoshan wasn't nuts enough to travel through the Jundland Wastes at night. They would pass the dark hours in the relative safety of the cave and start out again in the morning.

Which meant Luke had until morning to figure out how to escape.

"Is he asleep?" Jaxson whispered, just as Bossk's eyes fluttered shut. His scaly arms were wrapped tight around his blast rifle. Bands strapped around each leg were packed with flare pistol cartridges.

"You're alive!" Luke whispered back, deeply relieved.

"Of course." Jaxson sounded annoyed. "So how are we getting out of here?"

They were tied back to back, lying with Luke facing Bossk, and Jaxson facing the back of the cave. "If I could just get out of these," Jaxson mumbled, straining to escape from the restraints. But after a few minutes of struggling, he gave up. "No use," he muttered. "Looks like we're lizard food."

"Maybe not," Luke whispered. He couldn't reach his lightsaber. But maybe Jaxson could. "Can you reach around to my utility belt? On the right side?"

Jaxson wriggled in the restraints, fingers stretching toward the hilt of the lightsaber. "Almost —" he said, frustrated. "Can't — got it!"

Jaxson slipped the hilt out of Luke's belt. Luke twisted his hands toward Jaxson's and fumblingly groped for the lightsaber.

"Is it some kind of knife or something?" Jaxson asked.

Luke didn't answer him. The lightsaber was back in his hands. Now he just had to figure out what to do with it.

Activating the glowing beam with his hands tied behind his back would have been risky enough. But with Jaxson tethered to him, the risk doubled. If he sliced blindly, he could easily cut off one of their limbs.

But they had no choice.

Luke had done his best with the training exercises Obi-Wan had taught him. He'd spent hours in the forest, a blindfold across his eyes, using the lightsaber to deflect sting bursts he couldn't see. And every once in a while, he felt it, that mysterious connection to the Force. Every once in a while, the Force would guide his motions, and he would strike smoothly and surely, even with his eyes closed.

But that was practice.

"Don't move," he whispered.

"What do you mean?" Jaxson sputtered. "What are you going to do?"

Luke closed his eyes. He let the Force fill him. Then, in one swift motion, he activated the lightsaber and swiped it sharply to the right.

Jaxson rolled away, the cord binding him to Luke sliced neatly in two.

Another sharp twist of the glowing blade, and Luke's

wrists were free. It took only moments to free his ankles, and then he turned to Jaxson.

Jaxson's eyes were bulging. He shrank away as Luke came at him with the lightsaber, but allowed Luke to cut through his binders. "Where'd you get *that*?" he asked, reaching for it. Luke pulled the lightsaber out of his reach. He deactivated the Jedi weapon and slipped it back into his belt.

"Let's just get out of here," he whispered.

There was just one thing standing in their way. Or, more accurately, *sleeping* in their way. Bossk's scaly body lay across the opening of the cave.

"Just slice him open with that thing," Jaxson hissed. "He'll never see it coming."

Luke shook his head. He couldn't kill the bounty hunter in his sleep, no matter what the creature had done to them.

But he also couldn't beat the Trandoshan in a fair fight. Maybe a Jedi like Obi-Wan could have used the lightsaber to fend off a giant lizard and his blast rifle, but Luke knew he wouldn't have a chance.

Which left them with very few options.

"*Well?*" Jaxson looked almost ready to snatch the lightsaber and do the job himself.

Luke gazed at the airspeeder anchored just outside the cave. Then looked down again at the sleeping bounty hunter. "I think I have a plan."

*　　*　　*

Luke held his breath as Jaxson tiptoed over the slumbering Trandoshan.

Jaxson was right: it wasn't much of a plan, but it was all they had. As Jaxson crept toward the airspeeder, Luke stayed in the cave, his lightsaber activated. Its glowing blue tip hovered centimeters from Bossk's throat. If the bounty hunter was truly sleeping, Luke would wait for Jaxson to make it safely to the airspeeder, then dash after him.

But if Bossk was awake, lying in wait for his prey to make an escape attempt, then Luke would be there to stop him.

As Jaxson was halfway to the airspeeder, the Trandoshan's reptilian eye popped open. His clawed hand closed around the rifle.

"Don't," Luke said, holding his blade steady.

The bounty hunter laughed. "You think you can save yourself with a child's toy?" He swiped his arm toward the lightsaber, intending to knock it out of the way.

The blade cut cleanly through his limb. It dropped to the ground with a dull thud.

Luke stared in horror at the severed arm. Bossk didn't even flinch. He jumped to his feet, hissing with anger, and raised the blast rifle. Without thinking, Luke slashed at the rifle with his lightsaber, and the long barrel clattered to the ground. Enraged, the Trandoshan lunged for Luke. He danced out of the way, waving the lightsaber nearly at random to ward off the attack. Over Bossk's shoulder, he saw Jaxson racing back toward the cave — unarmed, yet determined to help.

"Go!" Luke shouted. "I can handle this!"

"Foolish last words, human," Bossk taunted, whipping out an archaic double-bladed sword. Luke had never seen one in person before — it looked ancient. Bossk brought the blade down over Luke's head. Instinctively, Luke raised the lightsaber to protect himself. The sword broke in half.

The look on Bossk's face would have been comical — if it hadn't been so terrifying.

The Trandoshan smashed a clawed fist into Luke's face. Luke went sprawling backward, but a moment later, he was on his feet again, hacking and slashing with the lightsaber. Bossk lunged for Luke, lashing out with his claws, but Luke dodged the blows. The glowing blade swept through the air, dancing around the Trandoshan. Luke wasn't thinking, wasn't aiming or strategizing, he just struck again and again, struggling and failing to land a blow. With a roar, Bossk hurtled toward him, wrapping his remaining hand around Luke's throat. Gasping for air, Luke slashed blindly with the lightsaber.

And then Bossk was on the ground. His left leg lay a meter away.

Luke gaped at his lightsaber, almost tempted to drop the deadly weapon on the ground, next to the writhing Trandoshan. It was almost like the lightsaber had taken over, fighting for itself.

And yet it had never felt so much a part of him.

"What are you waiting for, Skywalker!" Jaxson shouted, taking off toward the airspeeder. "Let's get out of here!"

Luke didn't need an invitation. He turned his back on Bossk and began to run. So he didn't see the wounded bounty hunter lob the fragmentation grenade with his one good hand. But Luke did see the deadly silver globe soar over their heads and land, with perfect aim, in the front seat of the airspeeder. "Down!" Luke shouted, grabbing Jaxson and throwing him to the ground, as the airspeeder exploded.

When the smoke cleared, Bossk was laughing. "Now we die together." He coughed, then spit out a gunky wad of viscous green blood. "Like I said — I always get the job done."

Han never felt quite right without his ship. The *Millennium Falcon* was docked in a shabby little hangar on Siskeen, where P'laang Ri, a Zabrak who owed Han more than a few favors, would look after it. The ship would be safe until Han returned, and the shuttle he'd borrowed was perfectly adequate. A scavenged *Zeta*-class Imperial shuttle, it was equipped with two double laser cannons and two double blaster cannons, along with a third, retractable rear-mounted double blaster cannon, just to discourage anyone who might want to follow. Not that they would need any of that, if everything went as planned, but it always helped to be prepared. Still, Han missed his ship. Right now, he especially missed the *size* of his ship.

The shuttle was large enough for two humans and a Wookiee to fit — but only if they pressed together, shoulder to shoulder. And, thanks to a burst hydraulics conduit at the beginning of their voyage, the whole cabin smelled like wet Wookiee fur. "Watch it, you dripping fuzzball!" Han complained, knocking Chewbacca's hairy arm out of his face for the hundredth time. He brought the shuttle into range of the Zoma satellite station and flicked on the comlink. Now they would either secure permission to board the station — or get blown out of the sky.

Either way, at least he'd get out of this shuttle.

"This is the shuttle *Arkanoid*," Han said into the comlink. "Requesting permission to dock."

"Transmit authorization codes, *Arkanoid*," came the impersonal response.

"You sure these codes are good?" Han asked Lore, who had purchased them on the black market.

Lore raised his eyebrows. "Don't trust me?"

Han wouldn't trust Lore to deal an honest hand of sabacc or play an honest round of four-cubes, and he certainly wouldn't trust his old friend around an open till. But when it came to plundering Imperial secrets, there was no one he'd rather have at his side.

Well, almost no one.

That's over now, Han reminded himself sternly. Luke, Leia, and the Rebellion were in the past, and he'd closed the door on that. A cargo of glitterstim and a good chunk of the credits he'd need to repay Jabba were his future — as long as he could get aboard the station.

Han transmitted the codes. A moment later, the station's tractor beam activated, sucking the shuttle into the docking bay.

"Welcome, *Arkanoid*," the voice said. "We've been expecting you."

"Maintenance crew down that way," the stormtrooper said, waving them down a long corridor. "Dump the Wookiee at the operations station with the rest of the furbags."

Chewbacca growled. He hated to be treated like an animal. But this was all part of the plan. Han had asked around and discovered that a team of Wookiees had been shipped in from the nearest prison planet to complete labor on the shield generators. From there, Chewbacca would be in perfect position to infiltrate the station's defense and weapons systems, ensuring that, if anything went wrong, the shuttle would make an easy escape. On a remote station like this, it seemed likely that security protocols would be lax enough to allow the Wookiee all the access he needed. Han prodded Chewbacca with his blaster. "You heard him, Wookiee. Let's go."

The stormtrooper shot him a sympathetic look. "You ask me, they may be strong, but they're not worth the trouble. Easier to wrangle a ship full of furnocs than get a good day's work out of a Wookiee."

"Tell me about it," Han said, as Chewbacca issued a long string of angry barks. Han suppressed a grin. No need to translate exactly what Chewbacca thought of this Imperial slug. Even a stormtrooper was likely smart enough to figure that one out on his own.

"Meet you in the cargo bay," Lore murmured, as Han escorted Chewbacca to the Wookiee labor unit. The Wookiee wore a thick, ill-fitting tunic that looked ridiculous but was loose enough to hide the bowcaster tucked beneath it. When the time came to leave, he'd hopefully have no trouble. "And we'll get to work."

The Imperials thought their newest maintenance team would be repairing the docking racks in the shuttle staging area.

But that wasn't exactly the kind of work Han had in mind.

Han had long ago learned that wearing a maintenance uniform was the key to getting pretty much anywhere you wanted to go. While high-profile visitors to an Imperial satellite station had to pass through any number of security checks as they wandered from one sector to another, no matter how important they were, maintenance workers quickly faded into the background. These days the Empire was doing so much construction work that most new projects were staffed by prisoners. There was little time or energy left over to guard the crews who kept the place running. No one cared what happened to the guy who fixed the plumbing or took out the trash. Which meant, thanks to their orange maintenance uniforms, no one gave Han or Avik a second look at they hurried away from the docking bay toward the aft cargo hold.

It had taken a good twenty minutes on the station's nearest computer terminal to determine where the shipment of glitterstim — confiscated from a rogue transport ship and en route to a legitimate distributor in a nearby star system — was stored. Not for the first time, Han found himself missing that annoying little astromech droid, who would have been able to ferret out the information in seconds. Still, they found it and easily slipped into the empty cargo hold. It was at least a hundred square meters in area and filled with stacks and stacks of shipping containers. There were no humans inside, only a few binary loadlifters, none of whom were sentient enough to note the presence of a couple unauthorized visitors.

"So far, so good, Chewie," Han said into his comlink. "Now we just need to dig up the shipment and we'll get out of here."

Avik dropped the two large tool cases he'd been carrying on the ground and flipped them open. Both were empty. Han glanced up at the giant piles of crates lining the walls of the cargo hold. He groaned. "This could take a while."

They began searching through the stacks, prying open one crate after another. Han found several cases of Whyren's Reserve (its amber color marking it as a particularly valuable vintage), kilograms of ionite (enough to retrofit the *Falcon* and several other ships), and a month's supply of bacta. But no glitterstim. They'd been at it for about fifteen minutes when the door to the cargo hold swished open. A stormtrooper in white armor clomped into the room, looking suspiciously back and forth between Han, Lore, and their empty toolboxes.

Han clambered off the crates of fusioncutters he'd been sorting through and ambled over to the guard. His hand strayed toward his blaster, but he kept calm. It was important not to act suspicious.

"What are you two doing in here?" the stormtrooper asked. "All maintenance crews were to report to sector seven."

Han shrugged. "No one told us, buddy," he said. "They sent us here." He jerked a thumb at Lore, who was fiddling with some exposed wiring in the far corner. "Told us we needed to repair the, uh, gyrostabilizers in the cargo lifts," he said, taking a wild guess at something that might need repairing.

The stormtrooper raised his comlink. "I'll have to check on that," he said.

"Don't bother," Han retorted, throwing all his weight against the stormtrooper and knocking him to the ground. The guard fumbled for his blaster, but Han knocked it out of his grasp. He reached for his own weapon. The stormtrooper lunged at Han, just as he was taking his shot. The laserfire went wild, crashing into a box of muja fruit. A geyser of bright red muja juice exploded into the hold. With a swift chopping motion, the stormtrooper smacked Han's blaster out of his hand, then headbutted him, hard. Han shook off the ringing in his ears to deliver a solid punch to the guard's stomach. But the white armor was impervious to the blow. "Little help here?" Han called to Lore, who was watching the fight, looking almost bemused.

"Sure," Lore said, as Han wrestled the stormtrooper to the ground, trying to pin him down long enough to reach for one of the fallen blasters. But every time he got the upper hand, the stormtrooper struck back, with a fist to Han's nose or an armored boot to his gut. And Lore was, inexplicably, taking his time. Out of the corner of his eye, Han saw him scoop up first the stormtrooper's fallen blaster, then Han's. Only then —

Han darted out of the way just in time — did Lore take his shot.

The stormtrooper went limp. His helmet slipped off, and Han, as always, experienced a moment of surprise to see the human face beneath the white plastoid mask. "Took you long enough," Han snapped at Lore. "But thanks."

"Don't thank me yet," said Lore, raising his blaster.

Han didn't have enough time to ask what he was doing.

Only enough time to think: *should have known better.*

And then Lore swung, hard.

The weapon struck the back of Han's head.

Lights out.

When Han woke up, he was propped against the wall of the cargo hold, his arms tied behind his back with a loop of fibra-rope. Lore was packing the final vials of glitterstim into the toolboxes. He smiled wryly at Han, without a hint of shame.

"Don't tell me this is payback for Dubrillon," Han said. He groaned at the sharp pain shooting through his head with every motion.

"Oh, please," Lore said. "This isn't personal, it's business."

"Someone trusses me up like a rong boar, I take that personally," Han warned him.

"Come on. Why split the payment in half when I can take it all? You'd have done the same thing, if I hadn't done it first."

"Never," Han said.

Lore laughed harshly. "Come on, Solo, you're the one who showed me the ropes in this game. Is it my fault you forgot the first thing you taught me?"

"Don't chew nerf steaks with your mouth open?"

"Trust no one," Lore said. "Look out for yourself, because no one else will." He grinned. "This must be a proud moment for you. The student surpasses the teacher." Moving quickly, he relieved the stormtrooper of his uniform, and then donned the armor himself. "Now, because we're old friends, you get a choice," he told Han, brandishing the stormtrooper's comlink. "I leave you for the Imperials to find . . . or I put you out of your misery, here and now."

"How about you untie me and we forget this whole thing ever happened?" Han suggested.

Lore didn't bother to respond.

Han ran out of patience. "Okay then, how about you take that blasted comlink and shove it in your frinking —"

"We have an intruder in the aft cargo hold, sector five," Lore said into the comlink, affecting the flat monotone of a stormtrooper. "Repeat. Intruder in aft cargo hold, sector five. Send reinforcements."

Moments later an alarm sounded, and the room lit up with flashing red lights.

Lore holstered his blaster, hoisted the tool cases, and slipped through the door, offering Han a farewell salute. "Remember, nothing personal!" he shouted over his shoulder.

"Nothing personal. Right. And I'm a gundark's uncle," Han grumbled, as a thunder of footfalls rumbled down the hall, and a sea of white armor flooded through the open door.

It looked like the reinforcements had arrived.

The stormtroopers yanked him to his feet.

"This is all a big mistake," Han said. "I'm just here to fix the cargo lifts."

"The cargo lifts don't need fixing," one of the stormtroopers responded, marching him into the corridor.

"All a big misunderstanding then," Han blustered. "No need to apologize. Just show me what needs fixing and I'll . . . uh . . . fix it."

This time the stormtrooper just ignored him, handing him off to two others. "Take the prisoner to interrogation," he said. They nodded in unison. Each grabbed one of Han's arms, and they marched him down the narrow white hallway.

Han had experienced Imperial interrogation tactics. He didn't have too much interest in a return visit. He wriggled around in his restraints. The stormtroopers had replaced Lore's makeshift rope cuffs with a pair of standard Imperial binders. There was no hope of escape, but if he stretched, he could *just* reach his comlink and open a channel to Chewbacca. Hopefully, Han could alert the Wookiee to the situation before he responded and gave the game away. "So, you're taking me in for an Imperial interrogation?" he said loudly, once he'd opened the channel. "Where is that, exactly?"

The stormtroopers ignored him. *Hope you're listening, Chewie,* he thought. There was the possibility Chewbacca had been taken prisoner as well. But Han didn't let himself think like that. The Wookiee was too smart.

Of course, so am I.

As they turned a corner, Han spotted the two things he needed for an escape: a notation marking this as corridor E-71, and a damaged bulkhead, its top half peeling away from the wall.

"See, you could use some maintenance after all," Han said loudly, hoping that Chewbacca could hear him — and that he'd succeeded in infiltrating the station's operating systems. Specifically, it's electrical system. "Look at that shoddy workmanship, right here in corridor E-71. That could be dangerous," he warned the stormtroopers. "What if you had some kind of electrical failure with your lighting system and someone just blundered into the bulkhead?" He shook his head, taking a close look around to memorize his surroundings.

The remote locking device for his wrist binders was tucked into the utility belt of the stormtrooper to his left. "Nothing more inconvenient than an on-the-job injury," he said. "You should really get that checked out. Now, while the lights are still on."

"What are you yammering about?" the stormtrooper on his right snapped irritably.

Come on, fuzzbrain, Han thought. *Get the message.*

But nothing happened. He'd have to buy himself some time.

Feigning clumsiness, he tripped and stumbled to his hands and knees. The stormtroopers stopped and hauled him back to his feet. "See, this is what I'm talking about," he said, even louder than before. "Imagine a bunch of clumsy folk bumbling around here in a *blackout*. Here in *corridor E-71*. You wouldn't want —"

The lights went out.

Han was ready. Before the stormtroopers knew what was happening, he slung his bound hands into the first one's head, knocking him into the second one. They tumbled to the floor together. By feel, Han found the locking device lodged by the stormtrooper's blaster, and then for good measure, snatched the weapon, too.

"See, fellas? This is what I'm talking about," he said, as he pried the peeling bulkhead off the wall. The stormtroopers were shooting blindly in the wrong direction, their laserfire sizzling through the dark.

* * *

"You said *right!*" Han hissed into the comlink, slithering backward through the duct until he reached the fork. This time, he took a left. Chewbacca growled into his ear. "No, if you'd said *left*, I would have gone *left*," Han snapped, inching forward again. He'd been shimmying through the ducts and conduits of the station for what seemed like hours, following Chewbacca's hastily whispered instructions. If all went according to plan, he'd eventually emerge in the shuttle docking bay, meet Chewbacca, steal a shuttle, and fly off to safety.

If he could ever find his way out of these tunnels.

This one passed right over a series of crew quarters, and the ceilings were thin enough that he could hear snatches of conversation filtering up from below. Banter about a recent game of zoneball, gossip about the latest antics of a well-known HoloVision star, even a parent yelling at his kid for shooting out a viewscreen with his junior blaster — it was almost easy to forget that this was an Imperial outpost, bent on rooting out the heart of the Rebellion and stomping it to pieces. They all seemed so normal.

And then:

"This is taking far too long!" an angry voice raged. "You know the punishment for failure."

"I have a lead," said another voice, strangely familiar. "Only a little more time and Skywalker is mine."

Though he knew the stormtroopers were tearing the station apart searching for him, and any delay could mean his life, Han froze.

One of the voices belonged to a stranger.

The other — it made no sense, but Han had no doubt — belonged to someone he knew and trusted. More to the point, someone *Luke* knew and trusted. It belonged to Tobin Elad.

X-7 couldn't avert his eyes from the screen. The Commander was terrifying in his rage. His narrow, pinched face remained palely inexpressive. But X-7 knew well the anger that roiled behind his steely eyes.

"You think you can escape?" *the Commander roars.*

X-7, who once thought himself a man without fear, cowers in the corner. A large borrat scampers toward him and begins gnawing at the flesh of his hand. X-7 ignores it. Locked in the dark for endless days, he has become used to the borrats.

"There is no escape from me," *the Commander says, quiet now. Dangerous.*

X-7 no longer knows how long he has been in the training facility. He no longer remembers how he came to be there. And he no longer knows who he once was.

But he knows he was someone.

Before they cleansed his brain, before they turned him into a machine to do their bidding, before he belonged to the Commander, he belonged to himself. He remembers that.

Which is why he killed the guards, scaled the walls, escaped.

Until the Commander's men dragged him back and threw him into the dark.

"You thought you'd succeeded, didn't you?" the Commander asks. He laughs. "I let you try. Wanted to see whether you'd make it."

X-7 is afraid to speak. He doesn't want to say anything that might make the Commander leave him alone again, in the silent dark. Any longer, and he fears he may go mad.

The Commander crosses the room, strokes X-7 gently across the forehead. X-7 shivers at the touch of another human, the confirmation that he is not alone in the galaxy. "This has been very hard for you," the Commander says softly. "I know. And you have a long road still to walk, my young friend. But at the end of it, you will emerge strong. I will make you strong. You want that, don't you?"

X-7 nods. He wants whatever the Commander wants. Because the Commander holds the keys to the door. The Commander can let him out of the dark.

"You're not going to try to escape again, are you?" the Commander asks. "You've learned your lesson, haven't you?"

X-7 nods again. He means it. But the Commander frowns. "No, you haven't," he says. "But you will. We'll make sure that you don't want to be anywhere else than here. That you don't want to do anything else but serve me. Only that will make you happy. You'd like that, wouldn't you?" he asks. "To be happy?"

X-7 nods.

"Speak, boy," the Commander snaps.

"Yes," X-7 says, hesitantly, his voice dry and raspy. It has been so long since he's spoken. "I want to be happy."

"And only one person can make you happy," the Commander says. "Do you know who that is?"

"You," X-7 whispers.

"That's good," the Commander says. He kneels down, eye to eye with X-7. He brings his face close enough that, in the dim light filtering through the open door, X-7 can see the rage in his eyes. The Commander pulls out a vibroblade, the light glinting off its razor edge. He presses it to the soft flesh beneath X-7's jaw. "Now then," the

Commander grits, bearing down."Let's teach you how to be happy."

X-7 recoiled from the rage in the Commander's gaze, glad that several light-years separated him from his master.

"Where is Skywalker?" the Commander asked, as he had been asking for the last several days. Each time, his voice grew quieter and tighter, as if a great force of will was needed to keep him from climbing through the screen and throttling X-7 with his bare hands.

Not that the Commander believed in applying his own force. He preferred a more elegant style of punishment.

X-7 suppressed a shudder. "Tatooine," he said, with a certainty he didn't feel. Extensive analysis of Luke's computer records had turned up traces of a deleted communication from several weeks before. An invitation to attend a gathering of old friends on his home planet, conveniently set for this week. There was no other evidence that Luke was there — along with no evidence whatsoever that he was anywhere else. It was X-7's best lead, and it would have to do.

"This delay is unacceptable, X-7," the Commander said.

"Yes, Commander," X-7 said obediently.

"You will go there now, and you will kill him."

X-7 nodded. "Am I still to maintain my cover as Tobin Elad?"

"If possible," the Commander said. "But your first priority is Skywalker's death. If you need to reveal yourself to do so —" His face wrinkled in distaste, and X-7 knew exactly what he was thinking. X-7 had been given a mission, and he had proven himself inadequate to the task. The Commander was now easing his standards. *If you need to reveal yourself* meant *If you're so incompetent that you can't do what I wanted you to do.* X-7 would pay for that later.

He was paying for it now, with a deep, throbbing pain radiating from his chest and head, so intense it was nearly paralyzing. The Commander had taught him well, and X-7's body remembered as well as his brain. The Commander's displeasure was X-7's agony, whether they were in the same room or halfway across the galaxy from each other.

"It will be done, Commander," X-7 said.

"And then you will report to me," the Commander said.

"That's not necessary —"

"You *defy* me?" the Commander asked in a level voice, raising his eyebrow. The ghost of a smile passed across his face.

"Never," X-7 said.

"Then when the job is done, you will report to me," he reported. "For further training. You seem to need a refresher."

Further training meant further pain. Meant further hours in the dark, with the needles and the blades. It also meant returning to the only place he would ever call a home.

"Yes, sir," X-7 said in a thin voice. "I look forward to it."

And deep down, in a dark, hidden corner of his mind, this was true.

The stormtroopers didn't know what hit them. They were expecting to find Han behind the bulkheads — not crashing through the ceiling of the shuttle bay, blaster blazing. He took down the two nearest stormtroopers before they had time to react. Chewbacca, storming in with two of the prisoner Wookiees on his heels, took care of the other six. Laserfire streaked across the shuttle bay, sparking and sizzling against the durasteel of the shuttle bodies. Alarms blared, but — as they'd originally planned before Lore's betrayal — Chewbacca had disabled the poorly protected shield systems that would have prevented an unauthorized departure. All they needed to do was select a shuttle, and they were good to go.

Han picked the ugliest of the ships, a *Lambda* with scarred wings and a gaping hole in the cargo unit. Something about it reminded him of the *Falcon*. And, he rationalized, if it had endured this much damage, it must be able to really *fly*.

"Whoa there," Han said, as the other two Wookiees tried to pile in after Chewbacca. "Where do you think *you're* going?"

Chewbacca growled, and gestured for the Wookiees to come inside.

"What do you *mean* they're coming with us?" Han asked, with a pointed look at the useless cargo hold and the cramped cabin. "Does it look like we have room for strays?"

Chewbacca growled again, pointing out that the Wookiees had helped him escape and now he was returning the favor.

Then he reminded Han that if it wasn't for his help, Han would be stewing in an Imperial interrogation chamber right about now.

Han sighed. He'd always had a soft spot for Wookiees. It couldn't hurt to help a couple of them break free.

Even if it would mean spending the return journey with a mouth full of fur.

*   *   *

"Well, what am I supposed to do, Chewie?" Han asked, leaning back in his chair. It should have felt good to be back on the *Millennium Falcon*, but something still felt off. A strange, queasy feeling, like everything was off-balance.

It's got nothing *to do with Luke and Leia*, he told himself. Probably he was still unsettled by Lore's betrayal, and the thought that once, he might have done the same thing.

Or maybe he'd just eaten some bad meatlump.

"You expect me to power up the hyperdrive and speed off to Tatooine?" Han asked. "All because I over-heard something that *may* mean Luke is in danger?"

Chewbacca's response made it clear this was *exactly* what he expected Han to do.

"You know who else is on Tatooine?" Han said. "*Jabba*. You realize that puts *my* life in danger, right?"

Chewbacca barked a dismissive reply.

"No, Jabba doesn't scare me," Han retorted hotly. "But he's got half the bounty hunters in the galaxy out looking for me — and you want me to show up on his doorstep? *Without* his payment?" Han shook his head. "Besides, don't you think it's just a little convenient that we stumbled onto exactly the information we were look-ing for? That of all the Imperial stations in all the galaxy we ended up on this one? A little *too* convenient, maybe?"

Chewbacca growled a final answer and, as if to make clear this was last word on the issue, turned his back on Han and began monkeying with the dented power cell housing.

"Don't know why you're so sure I'll do the right thing," Han muttered, staring blindly at the navigation computer, trying to decide which coordinates to enter. "Not like I ever have before."

I would know if Luke were dead, Leia kept telling herself. *I would know. I would know.*

Three words, repeated over and over again, got her through each moment and the next. They meant everything to her — and nothing to anyone else. As darkness fell, Luke's friends were ready to give up on him, but Leia insisted on staying and searching the area of the crash, seeking some clue to Luke and Jaxson's fate.

Of course, their broken skyhoppers were a clue. The fiery shards of durasteel were clues. The scorched desert, gashes in the ground, the smoldering ruins, all clues.

But not the kind of clues Leia was looking for.

While Luke's friends poked halfheartedly through the wreckage, already mourning the lost pilots, Leia and the two droids scoured the crash site.

Suddenly, R2-D2 beeped eagerly, twirling in circles on a patch of empty ground. C-3PO tottered over to him, then waved a golden hand at Leia. "Princess! Artoo says he's found something!"

Leia hurried over to the droids. "What is it?"

R2-D2 let out a long string of beeps and trills. C-3PO waved his index finger through the air. "Are you certain?" he asked the astromech. "We don't want to be too hasty —"

R2-D2 beeped indignantly.

"Of course you wouldn't be reckless at a time like this," C-3PO said. "I only meant that perhaps in your eagerness to help —"

R2-D2 cut in with a series of high-pitched, angry beeps.

"Fine," C-3PO gave in, and turned to Leia. "He says that he's picked up traces of an airspeeder, heading away from the crash site."

"Traces?" Leia looked around, seeing no telltale signs of any other vehicle. "What kind of traces?"

"Oh, patterns in the sand, trace amounts of baridium, any number of things," C-3PO said. "We droids are very sensitive to minor changes in the environment. Why, I once found a Zenji needle buried in a thirty meter high stack of —"

"Enough!" Leia snapped. "Can he track the airspeeder?"

R2-D2 beeped, then rolled a few meters toward the west. He paused, as if waiting for Leia to follow him.

"He says if we follow him, we'll find Master Luke," C-3PO said.

"Well, what are we waiting for?" Leia asked Luke's friends, as she hopped into the rusted landspeeder. "Let's go!"

Fixer and the others hadn't moved.

"What is it?" Leia asked impatiently.

"Those are the Jundland Wastes out there," Fixer said finally. "You don't know how dangerous they are. We'd have to be crazy to head out there at night."

"Luke would do it for you," Leia said.

"And I'd do it for him," Fixer said, "but . . ."

"But what?"

No one spoke. Fixer and Windy looked awkwardly at each other. Finally, Windy cleared his throat. "But we don't know that Luke and Jaxson are even out there," he said. "You have to admit, it doesn't make much sense. Where would an airspeeder come from out here? And why would Luke and Jaxson ride off on it?"

"That's what we're going to find out," Leia said.

"How?" Fixer asked. "By following your crazy droid?" He shook his head. "Look at this crash, Leia. I know you don't want to believe it, but —"

"They're not dead," Leia said firmly. "How many times do I have to tell you?"

"And we're supposed to trust you enough to risk our lives in the Jundland Wastes?" Fixer asked.

Leia shook her head in disgust. "Don't bother," she said. "I'll go myself. I don't need the help of a bunch of *cowards*." The droids clambered into the landspeeder, as she started the engine. "I assume you don't mind me borrowing this?"

Fixer glanced at Windy and Deak. Camie shook her head. "You can't," she told Fixer, pleading. "It's too dangerous!"

"I can't let her go out there by herself," Fixer said. He lowered his voice to a loud whisper. "And she called me a *coward*."

"I assure you, I'm quite able to take care of myself," Leia said indignantly.

"That's what you think," Fixer said. "You've never seen the Wastes." He jerked his head at Deak. "You ride back with Camie. Windy and I'll go with Leia."

"We will?" Windy asked. He looked nervously into the distance, where dark clouds billowed on the horizon, hanging heavy over the Wastes. Then he sighed. "I guess Luke'd do it for me. Let's go."

As they steered the landspeeder deeper and deeper into the desert, shadows played against the canyon walls. The unbroken stretches of sand, which had been blinding in the light of the setting sun, now faded into the night, as if the world ended in nothingness only a few meters away. The ground grew rockier, the landscape increasingly barren, but R2 claimed they were still on track, and so they pushed forward.

After they'd gone several kilometers, a warning light flickered on the landspeeder's instrument panel.

"The booster coils are failing," C-3PO said worriedly.

"That's it," Fixer said. "We have to turn around, head back before it shuts down completely."

"Artoo can fix it," Leia said calmly. "Can't you?"

R2-D2 beeped proudly.

"He says he can fix it," C-3PO translated, "but it could take some time."

"Just make it fast," Leia said, and slowed the landspeeder to a stop.

"We can't stop here!" Fixer yelped. "Are you nuts? The Sand People are everywhere. If they catch us . . ."

But Leia had already jumped out.

"Lady, you don't want to be wandering around here," Fixer said. "Not in the dark."

Leia reached into her utility belt and flicked on a small glowrod. The dim light illuminated the underbelly of the landspeeder. "It's not dark anymore," she said. "Let's get to work."

But there was little work for any of them to do, as

R2-D2 fiddled with the booster coils. Moments later, a high-pitched screech rent the air. Windy's eyes bugged out. "Krayt dragon," he whispered.

Another screech, louder and closer this time. It echoed through the canyons.

"Oh dear, oh dear," C-3PO moaned, diving into the landspeeder. "Don't just stand there, Artoo, climb in," he urged the little astromech. Together, they huddled beneath a tarp of coarse eopie hide and waited for disaster to strike. Windy and Fixer looked like they wanted to hide as well.

"There might be a cave over there," Windy said, gesturing toward the desert. "We could hide out 'til morning."

"We don't have time for that," Leia said. "Luke and Jaxson are out there somewhere. Unarmed."

"*We're* unarmed," Fixer pointed out.

"You are," Leia said. "I'm not." She pulled out her blaster.

Fixer held out his hands. "How about you let me handle that?"

"I don't think so," Leia said, as a keening howl shook the night. The krayt dragon lumbered out of the shadows. Leia froze. The last krayt she'd seen was just a baby, but this was a full-grown dragon, ancient and terrifying. A cloud of dust billowed in its wake as its massive paws pounded the sand. Windy and Fixer dove for cover behind the landspeeder, but Leia didn't flinch. As the dragon charged toward her, she steeled herself and took aim. The beast's thick scales would repel her blaster shots, but Luke had once told her that krayt dragons did have one small area of vulnerability: the sinus cavity. She scrutinized the creature's face, looking for the point between its crest of horns — each one easily as big as she was — and the bony armor of its dermal face plates. If she could aim her blast correctly, the laserfire would bore straight through the cavity and into the krayt dragon's brain.

The ground shook as creature closed in. Its jaws gleamed in the moonlight. Leia had time for one shot, and one shot only. She'd have to make it count.

Leia squeezed the trigger and a bolt of laserfire blazed across the darkness, smashing into the krayt dragon's sinus cavity. Its roar of rage tore through the night. It reared up on its hind legs and threw its head back, shrieking in pain. Leia readied the blaster for another shot. But it wasn't necessary.

With a final ear-piercing scream, the krayt dragon toppled over on its side. It heaved a great shudder, and then was still.

Windy and Fixer peeked their heads out, wide-eyed. "You *killed* it!" Windy said, sounding shocked. "By yourself!"

Leia was a little shocked herself, but she did her best

not to show it. Instead she just shrugged and holstered the blaster, like slaying unstoppable wild beasts was something she did every day. "Just a krayt dragon," she said, trying to stop her voice from shaking.

Windy and Fixer just gaped at her. There was something new in their expressions: respect. "You sure you're Skywalker's first mate?" Fixer asked.

Leia nodded. "Why do you ask?"

Fixer gave her a bashful grin. "Just seems like maybe *he* should be *yours*."

R2-D2 got the landspeeder running again and they picked up the trail without further incident. It was only a few kilometers later that they came upon the campsite, and the smoking wreckage of an airspeeder. They climbed out of the landspeeder, Leia flicking on her glowrod.

The airspeeder remains lay a few meters beyond a low-slung cave. And in the mouth of the cave: a body. Leia caught her breath for a moment, then let it out in a whoosh when she realized the body couldn't be Luke's. It was too large, for one thing. And as she drew closer, she could see its skin was covered in scales.

The body twitched.

Leia flinched. Then drew a step closer. Had she really seen a sign of life, or was it just a trick of the night? The creature was lying motionless, its arm and leg severed. Surely it couldn't still be alive. What kind of monstrous beast had left him in this condition?

"This is Jaxson's bag!" Windy shouted from behind her, holding up the tattered remains of a canvas sack. "And Luke's electrobinocs. You were right — they survived the crash somehow. They're alive!"

They're alive, and they were here, Leia thought, slowly turning in place and gazing out at the charred, vacant landscape. *But where are they now?*

CHAPTER FOURTEEN

Luke and Jaxson had agreed that they had the best chance of survival if they kept moving. It would be one thing if it was just a matter of making it through the night until rescuers arrived in the morning. Then they could wedge themselves into a cave and wait out the darkness. But there was no guarantee that anyone would come for them, no guarantee that they wouldn't have to spend another day and another night in the Jundland Wastes. They would have to sleep sometime, and it would be far safer to do so with the twin suns above the horizon.

It was about the only thing they could agree on.

"I told you this was the wrong way!" Jaxson hissed, as they trod through the dark and empty landscape. The glow of Luke's lightsaber led the way. "We should have gone *east*." Both had the skills to navigate by the stars. But knowing which direction you were heading didn't help without knowing where you started. And they had no idea how deep into the Wastes the bounty hunter had taken them — or in what direction home might be. Their only hope was to choose a direction and start walking, in hopes that in another few hours, or another few days, they would reach the border of civilization. They chose west, at random, knowing that choosing wrong would mean death. They had no food and no water, which meant a few days might be a few too many.

On the other hand, if they survived a few days in the Jundland Wastes, without getting eaten by a krayt dragon or besieged by Sand People, they would be lucky.

They would be lucky if they made it through the night.

"We just have to keep going," Luke assured Jaxson, with more confidence than he felt.

"What do you know?" Jaxson retorted. "You don't even live here anymore. Who are you to tell *me* what we should do?"

"You have a better idea?" Luke snapped.

There was a pause.

"Then we keep going," Luke said.

They walked several paces in silence.

"You got a problem?" Luke finally asked.

"Yeah," Jaxson spit out. "I'm stuck in the Jundland Wastes. In case you haven't noticed."

"I mean a problem with me," Luke said.

Jaxson just grunted.

"Because if you do —"

"I don't like traitors," Jaxson growled.

"But I told you —"

"And I don't like people who tell me what to think," Jaxson added, glaring at Luke. "Especially people who think they're better than everyone else, just because they can break orbit."

"I don't think I'm better than anyone," Luke protested.

"Coulda fooled me," Jaxson said, then quickened his pace so that Luke fell a step behind him.

Do I really act superior? Luke wondered. His eyes strayed to the lightsaber. Whenever he wielded it, he felt special, like there was something in him that was worthy, even powerful. He'd spent so many years feeling like a nobody, on a nothing planet — and then, to discover that he was *somebody*, a Jedi? Maybe the only Jedi left in the galaxy? He'd be crazy *not* to feel special.

But that didn't mean he thought he was better than anyone else.

Did it?

They walked briskly through the moonlit desert, trying to ignore their thirst and fatigue. The night had grown as cold as the day was hot, and Luke's fingers were growing numb. Gradually, a strange, unsettled feeling descended over him. For an instant, his senses clouded over, sheathing the world in shadow, and then the cloud dropped away, and everything was sharper, clearer than it had been before. Luke froze. He recognized that feeling.

Luke grabbed Jaxson's shoulder, gesturing for him to stop and stay silent.

Everything was thrown into sharp relief. The desert grit coating his skin, sandpapering his hands and face. The smell of the Wastes, a pungent mix of rot and death. The quietest sounds of the night screamed in his ears, separating themselves into discrete, recognizable units: the scurrying profroggs. Womp rats, feeding on a desiccated bantha corpse. And a shuffling sound.

Like footsteps, in unison, sweeping through the sand.

A muffled grunt, like the complaint of a bantha forced to carry a load heavier than it could bear.

Luke pressed himself against the wall of the nearby cliff, silently urged Jaxson to join him.

"What's wrong with you?" Jaxson hissed. "We have to keep going."

Luke shook his head.

The shuffling sound seemed to roar in his ears. How could Jaxson not hear it, not feel what was coming?

"Are you having some kind of fit, Skywalker?"

Sand People, Luke mouthed, then pointed over Jaxson's shoulder as the row of masked predators appeared on the horizon. Marching single file, each carrying a deadly gaffi stick and a rifle, trooping closer and closer to where Luke and Jaxson stood frozen, with no cover in sight. Jaxson's mouth formed a perfect "O" of horror. He threw himself against the wall of the cliff so hard it was as if he imagined he could bore through the stone with sheer will, lodging himself inside the rock until the danger had passed.

But unless the cliff magically swallowed them up, they'd be in plain sight when the gang of Tusken Raiders arrived. And, unarmed, they'd be an easy target.

Not unarmed, Luke thought. *I have my lightsaber.*

A lot of good it would do him against a horde of determined Sand People. Luke had heard rumors of the Tusken Raiders flaying their victims, tossing their corpses to the banthas. If he and Jaxson were here when the Sand People arrived, it wouldn't be a fight, it would be a massacre.

"We should run for it," Jaxson urged. "Now, before it's too late."

Luke shook his head. "It's wide open out there. They'll spot us, and then it's over."

"Like they're not going to spot us once they get

closer, and we're just sitting here like a couple of kriffing dewbacks?"

Luke didn't say anything.

"Well?" Jaxson pushed him. "You got a better idea? Because I'm not going to just stand here and wait to die."

You can't win, Luke remembered Ben once saying, *but there are alternatives to fighting.*

Luke hadn't understood it then, and he wasn't sure how it could help him now. He did know *exactly* what Han would have to say on the subject: *You don't need all that Jedi mumbo jumbo, kid. What you need is a good blaster.*

Han liked to claim that Obi-Wan's Jedi advice was impractical, useless in a real emergency. Luke always argued him, but right now, he was inclined to agree. Sure, Obi-Wan had been a master when it came to the Force, but what good was that when confronted with a band of angry Sand People who —

Of course! Luke thought, feeling stupid for not remembering sooner. He cupped his hands around his mouth and drew in a deep breath of air. Then, eyes closed, fingers mentally crossed, he blew out the best imitation krayt dragon call he could muster. And then he did it again, even louder.

"What are you doing?" Jaxson hissed angrily. "Now they'll come straight for us!"

"I don't think so," Luke said, nodding as the line of Sand People took a sharp turn toward the north, away from Luke and Jaxson's useless hiding place. In moments, they'd disappeared over the horizon.

Jaxson stared at him with wonder, the same expression that had crossed his face when he'd first seen Luke's lightsaber. "How'd you do that?"

"Tusken Raiders are afraid of krayt dragons," Luke said, trying not to shudder in relief that that trick had actually worked. "A dragon call is usually enough to scare them away."

"But how'd you know it would work?"

"An old friend of mine proved it to me, once," Luke said fondly. That had been the second time Obi-Wan had saved him in the Jundland Wastes. Years before, Obi-Wan had found Luke and Windy stranded in the desert, and led them to safety. The mysterious hermit had deposited Luke back at Uncle Owen's farm and disappeared into the wilderness. Luke hadn't seen him again until that afternoon Obi-Wan had saved him from the Sand People. So much had happened after that — learning that his father was a Jedi, burying his aunt and uncle, leaving Tatooine for a new life — he'd nearly forgotten.

I wish you were here with me now, Ben, Luke thought. The old man had lived in the Wastes for years — he must have learned a way to survive the harsh environment. But Ben was dead, and Luke was on his own.

Strangely, he didn't quite feel like it. Maybe it was because Obi-Wan had lived here for so long, or maybe it was because Obi-Wan's wisdom had, yet again, saved his life, but Luke felt the old man's presence. It was as if Obi-Wan was watching him every step of the way, urging him to go on, to survive.

Don't worry, Ben. I won't let you down.

As they pushed further west, endless stretches of flat desert gave way to a ragged landscape of cliffs and canyons. Luke and Jaxson found themselves edging along steep, gravelly paths in a darkness lit only by the blue glow of Luke's lightsaber.

"Where'd you get that thing, anyway?" Jaxson asked. "You steal it?"

"It belonged to my father," Luke said, inching along the narrow trail that wrapped around the cliffside. It had dwindled to less than a meter across, and beyond it lay a gaping chasm that seemed to stretch down forever. They'd searched for a path on more solid ground, but this was the only way through — so it was either edging along the cliffside or turning back the way they'd came.

"But you never had it before," Jaxson said.

"No," Luke agreed, reluctant to reveal any more details. "I didn't."

"So who's this Han Solo guy?"

"What?" Surprised to hear the name coming out of Jaxson's mouth, Luke whirled around, nearly losing his balance. His foot skidded across the gravel, and his body listed helplessly to the side. His arms pinwheeled, frantically searching for purchase.

His hand closed over a rocky outgrowth against the side of the cliff. He grasped it gratefully, heaving himself upright. The whole thing had happened in seconds. Behind him, Jaxson hadn't even noticed the near fall.

"How do you know that name?" Luke asked, once he was confident he'd regained his balance.

"Heard you and the Trandoshan talking about it," Jaxson admitted.

"I thought you were unconscious," Luke said.

"Yeah, well . . ." Jaxson hesitated, concentrating on his careful footsteps. "Figured it was better to lay low, see out what was going on. So who is he? Seems like I should know, since it's his fault we're here."

Who is Han Solo? Luke thought. That was the question, wasn't it? Not a killer, not an assassin, not a spy — and yet someone who would run away from an accusation, rather than staying to defend himself. Not a coward — and yet someone who would refuse to join the Rebellion's fight.

"He's a friend," Luke said simply. The answer felt right.

"Some friend, getting you into a mess like this," Jaxson grumbled.

"I'm sorry you got swept up in this," Luke said.

"Yeah. I heard what you said to the bounty hunter. About letting me go," Jaxson muttered, his voice nearly too soft to hear. "Guess I should say thanks."

Luke grinned." I never thought I'd hear you say — *ahhhhhhh!*"

This time there was no warning. One moment he was walking on solid ground — the next he was in the air. As the rock gave way beneath him, he had no chance to catch his balance, no hope of grabbing hold of something solid. Time seemed to slow, but the extra moments offered him no possibility of saving himself. They merely allowed him to experience every instant of the fall. His stomach lurched into his throat, the air rushed out of him, the stars brightened overhead, sharp and crystal clear and no doubt the last thing he'd ever see. And gravity, an anchor dragging him down and down . . .

A rough hand closed over his, yanking him upward. Luke felt like his shoulder was tearing in two, but he didn't let go. He tipped his head back. Jaxson was lying on his stomach, arm stretched over the side of the cliff, hanging onto Luke with a sweaty grasp. His hand slipped, and Luke squeezed tighter, fearing that the grit of sand between their skin was the only thing keeping him from plunging to his death. With his other hand, he scrabbled against the soft rock, trying to pull himself up, but it was no use.

"Hang on!" Jaxson shouted, straining to pull Luke back onto the trail. With a mighty heave, he managed to yank Luke up a few centimeters, not much, but enough that Luke could grab the edge of the cliff with the fingertips of his other hand. "Come on," Jaxson muttered through gritted teeth, panting with the effort. Luke mustered all his strength and, muscles straining, managed to raise himself up a little higher, enough to get a good grip on the edge of the rock. As he pulled himself up as hard as he could, Jaxson gave a final tug on his left arm, and dragged Luke back to safe ground.

For several moments, they just stared at each other, as if unwilling to believe it was over. "You can let go now," Luke said finally, and Jaxson dropped his hand. "You saved my life," Luke added.

Jaxson just shrugged. "Yeah. Well. Just watch your step next time."

Luke did. There were no more near misses, and no

more Tusken Raiders, nothing to break the monotony of the long, slow slog through the dark. And then, after several hours had passed, Luke became aware that he could see the shaded browns and tans of the sandstone cliffs, whereas before they had been nothing but looming shadows. The horizon lit up with a pinkish yellow glow. "We made it!" he said in wonder. "We survived until morning."

The relief died on his lips as the roar of an engine approached.

"The Trandoshan?" Jaxson gasped, looking pale. It was impossible — when they'd left, both the bounty hunter and his airspeeder had been in pieces. But who else?

"Luke!" a familiar voice shouted, as a red landspeeder came into sight. Leia leaned over the side, waving frantically. Windy was at the wheel, while Fixer and the droids waved from the back. Luke and Jaxson caught each other's eye and grinned. It was finally over.

They were safe.

Deep in the desert, something moved. Something cold and reptilian and left for dead. Something else that had survived the long night.

The hunter's red eyes flickered open. His remaining hand closed into a fist, claws piercing his scaly palm.

The wounds were deep, but they would heal. The arm and leg would grow back. Slowly, painfully, he would be whole again.

But it would take a long time to happen.

By the time it did, Bossk promised himself, Luke Skywalker would be dead.

nd then Leia just whipped out her blaster and blew that krayt dragon halfway to Coruscant!" Windy exclaimed, eyes bulging in appreciation. He gaped over Leia's shoulder at the other denizens of the cantina, as if shocked that they hadn't all gathered around to hear the amazing story.

Deak shook his head in disbelief. "Unbelievable. And you should have seen her at the crash site," he added. "She was fearless. We all thought you were dead, but she never gave up hope. It was like she *knew*!"

"And how about when we thought we saw the Sand People?" Fixer added. "No fear!"

"But it *wasn't* the Sand People," Camie reminded him irritably. "You said it was just the wind."

"Yeah, but if they *had* tried to attack us, Leia would've taken them down," Fixer said. He slapped Luke on the back. "That's some first mate you've got there," he said. "Maybe it's time to give her a promotion."

Luke caught Leia's eye, and grinned. The whole gang had ventured to Mos Eisley for a celebration of Luke and Jaxson's survival — but the night was quickly turning into a celebration of Leia's bravery. And Leia looked just fine with it. The princess usually spurned flattery and wriggled uncomfortably out from under the spotlight. But this was different, she'd confided to Luke in a quiet moment. "They don't respect me for being a princess or a Senator," she'd told him. "Just . . ."

"For being you?" Luke had filled in when her voice trailed off. "Good. They *should*."

And it's not like Luke was being ignored. At least no one was calling Luke "Wormie" anymore, or questioning whether he was *really* a rogue hotshot pilot. They were willing enough to believe that his daring had let him do the impossible: survive a night in the Jundland Wastes.

But Luke preferred to sit back quietly and listen to his friends swap stories. It was strange, being back in Mos Eisley for the first time since he'd blasted off from Tatooine with Han and Ben. So much in his life had changed — and yet the city was the same cesspool of vice and corruption it had always been.

Fixer had been the one to suggest that they make

this celebration something special, not just the same old tired game at Tosche Station. The rest of the gang had been quick to agree — all except for Luke. He told himself he was wary of the Imperial garrison in the center of town, and of the concentration of bounty hunters and other criminals under Jabba's thumb.

But the real reason: He didn't want to return to the place where he and Ben had first met Han Solo. And to remember that both of them were gone from his life now, probably forever.

He was overruled.

It had taken several hours to reach the city, and another one to make their way through crowded streets teeming with bazaars and marketplaces, pushing past moisture farmers toting their wares, grizzled spacers awaiting their next mission, aliens from every corner of the galaxy huddling in corners, exchanging secrets in hushed tones. The air was fetid with the stench of the dewbacks, eopies, jerbas, and rontos that packed the street, carrying their weary travelers from one cantina to the next.

And there were plenty of cantinas. That was one of the things about Mos Eisley that would never change. Deak had suggested Chalmun's — but only as a joke. The spot was famous for its rowdy crowd, underground warrens of vice, and frequent blood sport. Luke decided not to mention that he'd once passed an afternoon inside, only to come very close to death by way of an angry Aqualish.

Instead, they settled on Pisquatch's Place, a snug cantina a few blocks down from Chalmun's on Outer Kerner Way. With only one room, five drink options, no live music, and a crowd filled with touchy young wannabes — aspiring pilots rubbing shoulders with aspiring criminals — the Place had only one thing in common with Chalmun's Cantina: no droids allowed.

So C-3PO and R2-D2 waited outside, while Luke fended off his friends' demands for details about how he and Jaxson had managed to survive a night in the Jundland Wastes. There was no reason to keep it a secret, but Luke — who had already told so many tales of his fake life as a space smuggler — didn't relish making the experience into another adventure story. And, although they hadn't discussed it, Jaxson seemed just as reluctant. No one knew about how Luke's lightsaber had freed them from the bounty hunter, or that Jaxson's quick reflexes had saved Luke from toppling over a cliff. But the latter wasn't something Luke would soon forget. As his friends pestered Leia, clamoring for more details of her adventures in space, Luke pulled Jaxson aside. They retreated to a quiet corner of the cantina, pausing beneath a garish painting of Noosh Feteel, one of Mos Eisley's founding fathers.

"What is it?" Jaxson asked, looking like he could guess, but was hoping to be wrong.

"I just wanted to thank you again," Luke said. "For what you did out there."

Jaxson shrugged. "Yeah, well. Whatever."

"You saved my life!" Luke said.

"Yeah." Jaxson shifted his weight uncomfortably. "I remember."

"I guess I owe you one," Luke said. "And listen, what I said before, about your piloting?"

"You mean, like how I had the hand-eye coordination of a blind womp rat?" Jaxson said sourly.

Luke flushed. He didn't remember using *exactly* those words. "Right. That. I didn't mean it. You're good — good enough that they should have let you into the Academy. But listen, it's really a good thing they didn't. Biggs —"

"You going to start up with that trash again, Skywalker?" Jaxson snarled. "Going to tell me that I'm lucky I didn't ship out to the Academy, because then I might have ended up serving in the big, bad Imperial Navy?"

"I was just —"

"Look, maybe I was wrong about you, too, Wormie," Jaxson admitted. "Maybe you're not just out for yourself. Maybe you don't think you're better than the rest of us. But last night doesn't change the fact that Fixer was right. Doesn't matter who's in charge of the galaxy, as long as the vaporators keep running."

Luke used to think the rest of the galaxy had nothing to do with Tatooine, too. Until the day the Empire arrived and slaughtered his aunt and uncle. That was the day Luke had realized that the Empire's reach was everywhere. But he knew he wouldn't be able to convince Jaxson of that, or any of them. It was something they'd have to figure out for themselves. And part of Luke hoped they would never have to. Life on Tatooine was hard enough.

He held out a hand for Jaxson to shake. "Then just thank you. I owe you my life."

Jaxson cocked an eyebrow at Luke, looking for a moment remarkably like Han. "Don't worry about it, Wormie. You'll pay me back some —"

A crash of transparisteel cut off his words. Luke spotted the telltale gleam of a blaster barrel and, before he even processed what it meant, threw himself at Jaxson, knocking both of them to the ground. A searing blast of laserfire flew through the air where their heads had been, striking the ugly painting behind them. A jagged hole exploded in the Mos Eisley forefather's forehead.

The creature in the doorway held the blaster in his right hand and as he stepped fully into the cantina it became clear that his left arm ended at his shoulder in a cauterized stump. His scaled face was bruised and dented, and one red eye clouded over with green blood. He lurched through the door on one leg, and swung the blaster across the cantina, spraying laserfire in every direction.

Bossk was back.

ey — he's supposed to be dead!" Luke protested, as he overturned a table and pulled down Leia behind it for cover.

"I guess no one told him," Leia said, her blaster already in hand. She peeked her head out and took a couple shots. Laserfire erupted all around them, and she lowered her head again, safely shielded behind the table. Luke spotted Jaxson, Windy, and Fixer cowering beneath another table a few meters away. None of them were armed.

"Jaxson!" Luke shouted. When Jaxson turned, Luke tossed him his blaster.

"What are you doing?" Leia asked.

"I have my lightsaber," Luke said. "That'll be enough."

He raised his eyes above the edge of the table, just enough to scope out the situation. Bossk, who had attached the sawed-off barrel of a blast rifle to the charred stump of his left leg, was framed in the doorway, his own blast rifle peppering the cantina with laserfire. His two allies, the Gamorreans who had blasted through the windows, stood in opposite corners of the cantina, firing at anything that moved.

But this was Tatooine, which meant plenty of the cantina patrons were ready and willing to fire back. Every time Bossk and the Gamorreans tried to advance, they were pinned down by a barrage of laserfire. So they stayed at the perimeter, deflecting shots with chairs and tables, pinning down everyone who lay inside. It was a "Mos Eisley" standoff.

The room was thick with smoke. A foul stench of scorched plastoid hung heavy in the air. Shards of sunlight filtered into the dark room through shattered transparisteel, lighting up the pale, terrified faces of the unarmed cowering behind furniture.

A hammerheaded Ithorian leapt up from behind the long bar, emitting a keening wail as he raced toward the exit. He made it ten steps before blasterfire cut him down, and he dropped to the ground in a twitching, moaning heap.

Luke tightened his grip on his lightsaber. *Enough.* The bounty hunter was here for *him*, and he wasn't about to hide under a table while innocent people were hurt.

"If you and Jaxson can take out the Gamorreans, I can handle Bossk," Luke told Leia. She gaped at him.

"You don't even have a real weapon!" she protested.

"Just trust me," Luke said. "We have to end this now."

Leia glanced over her shoulder at the nearest Gamorrean. "He's not covering his right flank," she said. "I think I can take him down, if I can make it over in that direction. And if Jaxson can get the other one."

Luke caught Jaxson's eye, and jerked his head toward the Gamorrean at the far end of the saloon, who held a heavy blaster in one hand and a disrupter rifle in the other. Every few seconds he fired off a warning shot. When he got bored of that, he played target practice with the row of bottles lining the bar, exploding them one by one. If Jaxson could make it to the edge of the room, and sidle along the wall unseen, he'd have the perfect angle for a direct hit. Jaxson followed Luke's gaze, then gave him a confident nod.

On my signal, Luke mouthed, and, nodding again, Jaxson began to inch into position.

"You sure you know what you're doing?" Leia whispered. Luke nodded. She squeezed his shoulder, then slipped away.

"Bossk!" Luke shouted, hoping to draw attention away from his friends as they lined up their shot. "It's me you want! Leave these people alone."

"The coward speaks," Bossk said, then aimed a round of laserfire at Luke's head. Luke ducked below the table again. Once Leia and Jaxson took out the other two shooters, it would be easy to dispatch Bossk. But Luke didn't want him dead. Not until he found out who'd hired the bounty hunter. "Surrender yourself, and we can end this."

"How about you surrender *your*self," Luke suggested, trying his best to channel Han's confidence. "Unless you want to lose the *other* leg."

The bounty hunter chuckled. "You plan to take on a Trandoshan and two Gamorreans?"

"I'm not worried about the two Gamorreans," Luke said — and, simultaneously, Leia and Jaxson took their shots. The snout-nosed aliens fell in unison, with a single, resounding thud. Luke leapt to his feet. "Leave the Trandoshan!" he shouted to the cantina. "He's mine."

Bossk chuckled again, although this time his laughter sounded hollow. He pulled the trigger on his blast rifle, sending a blast of laserfire directly at Luke's chest. Without hesitating, Luke blocked it with his lightsaber. The laserfire ricocheted off the glowing blue blade, and Luke advanced toward the bounty hunter.

It's just like I practiced, Luke told himself, as Bossk blasted away at him. Luke whirled the lightsaber through the air, deflecting shots one after the other.

Focus, he thought.

Concentrate.

Let the Force guide you.

This time it wasn't just Obi-Wan's voice that he heard. It was as if Obi-Wan himself was present, guiding Luke's hand. The lightsaber zigzagged with a smooth surety and grace that Luke had never before achieved, even in his best training sessions. The glowing blade shimmered and sparked as the blasts pinged off of it and, step by step, Luke advanced on the Trandoshan. The cantina had fallen silent, every eye on Luke and his dancing blade. Finally, Luke was close enough to slash the blaster out of the Trandoshan's had.

Close enough to make good on his promise to take the Trandoshan's other leg — if he wanted to. Which he didn't. The thought of such a brutal act, even in self-defense, made him sick. But he had to hope that Bossk believed he was capable of it.

The Trandoshan reached for the BlasTech pistol tucked into his belt. But Luke stopped him with a flick of the lightsaber. "You're stronger than me," he said quietly. "You may even be faster than me. But you've seen what this weapon can do." He touched it to the Trandoshan's armored breastplate. "This can slice through your armor in an instant. You may be able to survive without an arm or a leg, but can you survive without a heart?"

"I will not beg for mercy," the Trandoshan said coldly.

"Slay me if you must. The Scorekeeper will embrace me with honor for my many kills." Luke knew he believed it. Bossk didn't fear death. He feared cowardice, humiliation, and dishonor. The crueler punishment would be to let him live.

"Who are you working for?" Luke asked.

Bossk's jaws drew back in a jagged smile. "There's only one creature on this dung heap of a rock who's worthy of my services. One creature who owns you all."

Jabba. Of course.

"Then go back to your employer, and you tell him it doesn't matter how many bounty hunters he sends after me. I'll *never* help him get Han."

"You would die to protect that spacer scum?" Bossk asked.

"No one's dying today," Luke said. But if it came to that? Yes. And Luke knew that Han would do the same for him. No matter what had happened, Luke was sure of it. "So while you're at it, you can give Jabba another message: You want Luke Skywalker? Better come and get him yourself. If you *dare*."

Luke knew his message would never get back to Jabba. The Trandoshan would probably hop the first freighter off the planet, rather than face Jabba's wrath at having failed. Or he would try again, round up another handful of incompetent Gamorreans for another attempt on Luke's life. But — Luke watched the Trandoshan hobble away — he doubted it. And even if the bounty hunter decided to try again, by that time, Luke would be long gone. He was done hiding out; and he was done pretending that this was a place where he still belonged.

It was time to go home.

-7 peered through the scope of his A280 longarm blaster rifle, watching Luke and his friends dodge blasterfire. His hand tightened on the front-grip pump as he readied for the shot. From his perch on the roof of an out-of-business water distribution plant across the street, he had a perfect view of the chaos inside the cantina. Tatooine's blazing suns blanketed him with a brutal heat that radiated in waves off the bleached pour-stone of the roof. Sand coated his hands, his face, the insides of his nose and mouth. It was as if the desert was consuming him. This place was the armpit of the galaxy, and the sooner he got out, the better. But he couldn't go anywhere until Skywalker was taken care of.

He waited impatiently for the Trandoshan to deal Luke a death blow. But it never came. And X-7 found himself relieved. Which made no sense. It shouldn't have mattered whether Luke died by X-7's hand or the bounty hunter's claw. All that should have mattered was that the target ended up dead, and the Commander was satisfied. Fulfilling the mission, that was to be his only job, his only care.

But this time, X-7 wanted more than that. He *wanted* the kill. Luke had defied him one too many times, clinging to life; Luke had made the Commander doubt X-7's competence. Luke Skywalker needed to die, and X-7 needed to be the one to make that happen.

X-7 knew something was wrong. He wasn't supposed to feel *want*. Just as he wasn't supposed to feel frustration, or impatience as he watched the battle play out, his finger itching on the trigger of his blaster. These were emotions — and emotions were dangerous. More than that, they were forbidden.

X-7 also knew that he should report his problem to the Commander, who would be further convinced it was time for more training. More time in the box, pinned to the wall, pincers prying through his thoughts and memories, cleaning him out. Or perhaps the Commander would decide he wasn't worth the trouble and terminate him. This shouldn't have mattered, either. Life was nothing to X-7, nothing but a way to serve the Commander. If he could better serve the Commander through death, so be it.

But nothing was the way it was supposed to be, not since Luke. The longer he spent on this mission, the more he wanted to complete it. And the more he *wanted* other things, whether or not he was supposed to. Things like Luke's death.

Things like his own life.

Everything will get back to normal, he told himself. *Once Skywalker is dead.*

The wounded Trandoshan limped out of the bar. X-7 had no idea why the bounty hunter would have given up before he or his target was dead. But it wasn't important. It was X-7's turn now. Luke was standing behind the shattered window, jagged transparisteel framing his trusting face.

Kneeling, X-7 rested the barrel of the blaster on the edge of the roof, and framed Luke's head in the targeting scope. He lined up the perfect shot. His finger tightened on the trigger, but he hesitated. Just to savor what was to come. Just a moment — but a moment too long.

The blast nozzle jabbed hard into the back of his head. X-7 likely would have been able to identify it by feel — a DL-44 heavy blaster — but he didn't have to. He knew exactly what kind of blaster it was, because it was accompanied by a familiar voice.

"Drop it." Han didn't wait for X-7 to comply. He kicked the weapon out of X-7's hands. It toppled off the roof, crashing into a Jawa trading post below and clanging against an unsuspecting R2 unit. The unit beeped and sparked, skidding wildly toward a tethered eopie. The spooked beast reared up on its hind legs, slamming back to the ground squarely atop a stall of fresh pallie and pika fruits. A clutch of angry Jawas and fruit vendors gaped up at the roof, shouting in squeaky voices and shaking their fists.

"Get up," Han ordered. "Slowly."

As he climbed to his feet, X-7 did some quick calculating. He could kill Solo now — the smuggler's blaster was nothing against X-7's speed and K'tara fighting skills. But he couldn't do it now, not with half of Mos Eisley watching from below. His orders had been to remain undercover for as long as possible, to kill Luke without losing the Rebellion's trust. Which meant he would have to let this play out as long as he could, and try to turn it to his advantage.

"Better shoot me now, Solo," X-7 growled. "At least if you want to live past sundown." No point in denying what he really was, not when he'd been caught in the act.

Han shook his head. "You're no good to me dead," he said. "Not until we make it good and clear to *our* friends what you've been up to. You want to quit breathing after that? Be my guest."

X-7 laughed. "You came all the way here to clear your name? How . . . *cute.* Too bad it'll never happen."

Han just scowled at him, and raised his comlink. "Chewie, how's it coming down there?"

The Wookiee barked in response, and Han nodded sharply. "Well, hurry it up." He kept the blaster steadily aimed at X-7. "*Our* friends will be here soon."

X-7 smirked. "Just in time to rescue their good and loyal friend Tobin Elad from the diabolical Han Solo."

"They're going to find out exactly what their *good and loyal friend* is made of," Han snarled.

"And you've brought evidence, have you?"

Han said nothing.

X-7 arched an eyebrow. "Your word against mine, then?" he said. "The word of a man who stashed several kilograms of detonite in his quarters? Who fled justice, rather than face his accusers? The man so scurrilous that even Jabba the Hutt has deemed him untrustworthy? I'm sure *our* friends will have no trouble believing a man like that."

X-7 could read people; it was the only way he'd stayed alive for so long. So when Han lowered his eyes and said, quietly but firmly, "*I'm* sure," X-7 knew.

He wasn't.

"But where's Han?" Luke asked, yet again, as Chewbacca led them through the Mos Eisley crowds.

"And what are you doing on Tatooine? What's going on?"

Chewbacca just issued the same terse bark he had every time Luke asked.

"He says, 'You'll see,'" C-3PO translated, sounding rather displeased. They threaded their way through a cluster of chattering Jawas, standing in the midst of a pile of spare parts and smashed pika fruits and shaking their fists at the sky. "Listen to me, you Wookiee —"

Chewbacca cut him off with a warning growl.

"I'm merely suggesting that if you were to offer us some additional information about what you and Captain Solo are doing on the planet, we might be in a better position to help," C-3PO huffed.

The Wookiee ignored him, disappearing into an empty water distribution plant and beckoning them to follow. He hurried to a dark, crumbling stairwell and rushed up the steps, two at a time.

R2-D2 beeped.

"What do you *mean* we can trust him?" C-3PO asked. "Do you know how many times he's threatened to tear my arms off?"

R2-D2 beeped again.

"*Yet?*" C-3PO yelped. "He hasn't done it *yet*? Is that supposed to make me feel better?"

Luke and Leia brushed past the droids. They were

wasting time. "Come on," he urged them. "Something's going on. Let's see what it is."

Luke followed Chewbacca all the way up the roof. And when he stepped out of the stairwell, he stopped so abruptly that Leia nearly slammed into him. "What is it?" she hissed.

Luke didn't respond. He just grinned.

"Good to see you're still in one piece, kid," Han said. Then he inclined his head toward Leia. "Greetings, Your Worshipfulness."

Leia's eyes widened. "Han! I can't — what are you doing up on the . . . ?"

But she swallowed her words as Han stepped aside and revealed the figure kneeling by the edge of the roof, Han's blaster digging into the side of his head.

"Elad!" Luke exclaimed. "What's going on?"

"What's going on is that you owe me another one, kid." Han grimaced down at Elad. "Everything he's told you is a lie. He's not here to help you — he's here to kill you."

Luke shook his head. Tobin Elad had become a good friend. He'd listened when Luke needed to talk. He'd believed in Luke when Luke hadn't had the strength to believe in himself. "The explosion on Yavin 4?" he asked quietly. "You're saying . . ."

"He's a spy," Han said. "Working for the Empire."

"How do you know?" Leia asked.

Han raised his eyebrows. "What if I told you I just knew?" he asked. "What if I told you to trust me?"

Elad turned his face toward Luke and Leia for the first time. "Don't listen to him," he said, in a firm, steady voice. There was no trace of fear in his eyes. "*He's* the Imperial spy. He came here to kill you, Luke. It's why I'm here — to stop him."

Han jabbed Elad with the blaster. "Shut up."

"Or what?" Elad asked. "You'll kill me in cold blood? That will only prove the truth: that you're a mercenary. For enough money you'll do anything. Even kill an innocent man. Or —" He glanced meaningfully at Luke. "Someone foolish enough to believe he's your friend. If I have to die to reveal who you really are? So be it."

"You're not listening to this junk, are you?" Han asked. "You barely know this guy. Don't know anything about him. And you're going to believe him over me?"

"And what do they know about you?" Elad countered. "Other than the fact that you're a smuggler, a criminal, and wanted in twenty different star systems. Go on," he urged Leia. "Ask if he has any evidence. Ask if he has a shred of proof that *I* would ever be a threat to the Rebellion."

Leia didn't even hesitate. "He doesn't need any."

Han started in surprise. "I don't?"

"He doesn't?" X-7 said, his surprise shocking even himself.

"No," Luke answered for her. "He doesn't."

The certainty that filled him had nothing to do with the Force. He didn't need the Force to tell him that he could trust Han. The pilot had proven his loyalty, and his friendship, again and again — and no matter what had happened on Yavin 4, that was unquestionable. Luke had come to Tatooine hoping to take comfort in the friendships of his past, people he'd known long enough and well enough that their loyalty could never be questioned.

But coming home had made him realize that he wasn't the same naïve moisture farmer he'd been when he left. He wasn't the same Luke Skywalker who'd hunted womp rats with Windy and matched daredevil skyhopper maneuvers against Fixer and Jaxson. They'd known him longer, but they didn't know him better. Not anymore.

Luke had only known Leia and Han for a short time, but they were more than friends, they were family. And he trusted them both with his life.

He gazed steadily at the man who'd called himself Tobin Elad. "If Han says you're a threat, then you're a threat. All I need is his word."

Han broke into a surprised grin. "Then I guess you won't be wanting this?" he said, and tossed a datacard in

Luke's direction. Luke snatched it out of the air and looked at it in confusion.

"Holorecording of the spy getting orders from his boss," Han explained. "Ask most people, and they'd tell you my word isn't worth two credits."

Elad looked disgusted. "You're all fools," he snapped. "And it's going to be my pleasure to kill you."

"Not today," Luke said, amazed by the transformation. In seconds, Elad had become a stranger — his voice, his posture, even his *face* seemed different. Harder. Crueler.

"No," Elad said. "But soon." And then, with lightning speed, he slashed an arm out, slamming into Han's windpipe. As Han gasped and lurched forward, Elad sprang to his feet and leapt off the edge of the roof.

Luke rushed forward in time to see Elad's falling body reverse motion in midair and rocket toward the sky. Smoky plumes billowed from his hidden jetpack as he sailed over the roofs of Mos Eisley.

"Can't believe I let him get away," Han muttered angrily as soon as he could breathe.

"Don't worry." Luke watched Elad's figure dwindle to a speck, disappearing on the horizon. "He'll be back."

o, why'd you come back?" Leia said coolly, once enough time had passed that it was clear the escaped assassin wasn't returning. "Finally get bored playing your little space games?"

"Games?" Han repeated in disbelief. "*Games?* I risk my *neck* to come back here and save your lives — even after you accused me of trying to blow up Luke — and *that's* the thanks I get? Maybe I should have just stayed away."

"Maybe you should have," Leia snapped. "Then you wouldn't have to explain why you ran away in the first place."

"Listen, sweetheart, no one said anything about running away." Han jabbed his finger in the air toward her. "For all you know, I only busted out of there so I could find out who was after Luke."

Chewbacca interrupted with a nagging bark. Han waved him off.

"See, now you've hurt Chewie's feelings," he said. No need to translate what the Wookiee had *actually* said. "That's some thank you."

Luke cleared his throat. "Thank you, Han."

"*You're* welcome, kid," Han said, shooting a glare at Leia to make sure she knew she wasn't included in the sentiment.

"I still don't get how you knew Elad was a spy," Luke said. "Or how you knew we were here. Or —"

Han waved away the questions. "Long story."

Chewbacca let loose a long stream of growls and barks.

"What's he saying?" Leia asked.

Han shook his head. "Don't mind him; the fuzzball here's just hungry. Gets a little testy when he misses dinner."

C-3PO cleared his throat. "If you'll pardon me, Princess, the Wookiee has explained that Captain Solo located the truth at grave risk to his own life!"

Leia quirked her lips into a half smile. "Is that true, Captain Solo?"

"It might be."

"Then I offer you my sincerest gratitude on behalf of the Rebellion," she said formally.

Han gave her a deep mock bow. "On behalf of myself, I accept."

"And Han —" The icy distance was gone from her voice, along with any trace of mockery. "Thank you. Han . . . I'm sorry about before. On Yavin 4. That should never have happened. We should have trusted you."

Han shrugged, as if it didn't matter. "You did what you had to do, Princess. Just like the rest of us."

Luke shook his head. "But we knew all along that you never would have —"

Leia put a hand on his shoulder to stop him. "No. It was my call — it was my investigation. And . . ." She steeled herself again. "I'm just glad you came back. The Rebellion needs you."

"Well, if the *Rebellion* needs me," Han said, giving her a knowing grin. You *need me, too, Your Worshipfulness*, he thought. *And one day you're going to admit it.* "I guess I'll stick around a little longer. Give you plenty of time to make it up to me." He cast a sharp glance over the roof, where the fruit vendors had righted their stands and the Jawas had gotten back to work, peddling half-defective droids and bartering with locals for their credits. A couple of them were still staring up at the roof, looking far too interested in what they saw there. "How about if you do the rest of your groveling back on the *Falcon* — Jabba's going to hear I'm back in town, sooner or later. And by the time he does, I plan to be halfway across the galaxy."

"Not that you'd ever *run away*," Luke teased.

"Hey, kid, there's running away, and then there's *being smart*. You want to stay alive much longer? You'll figure out the difference."

"I think I'm beginning to understand," Luke grinned at his friend. "But before we go, let's attend the services for Biggs — that's why we came, right?"

Feeling as good as they had since the award ceremony following the destruction of the Death Star, Luke, Solo, Leia, Chewbacca, and the droids left the roof and melded into the crowds of Mos Eisley. They headed toward a cemetery in the desert where they would make it just in time to pay their last respects to Luke's childhood friend and a hero of the Rebellion.

"Another chance?" Jabba the Hutt reclined in his throne, gulping down a live, wriggling gorg coated in spicy mubasa sauce. "HO! HO! HO!" His massive body shook with each burst of gurgling laughter. "You want another chance to fail me?"

The Trandoshan bounty hunter strained in the grip of the Gamorrean guards who held him in place, still angry about the wasted deaths of their brothers-in-arms. Struggling was useless; the guards held him with a durasteel grip. "The human was setting a trap for you," Bossk told Jabba. "He *wanted* to be captured. You should be thanking me."

"HO! HO! You saved me from a *human*?" Jabba laughed again, and the rest of his court hastily joined him. "Then why did you try to sneak off-planet in the middle of the night like a Baldavian pocket hare? Why not come to me and claim your reward?"

"I will get Skywalker for you," Bossk hissed. "And Solo. And" — he pounded a clawed fist against his armored chest — "the *Wookiee*. They're mine."

"They're *mine*," Jabba roared. Alarmed by the sound, the Kowakian monkey-lizard who played court jester plunged his head into a nearby vat of boga noga. "Just like everything else on this planet," Jabba added. "Perhaps you need a reminder of that."

Bossk shook his head.

"What do you think?" Jabba asked the room. It erupted into hooting cheers. A storm of voices whirled around them, but one word became clear, chorused over and over again. *Rancor.*

Jabba nodded. "Step forward for your *reward*, bounty hunter."

The Trandoshan stayed rooted to the floor until the Gamorreans pushed him forward.

"Have no fear, bounty hunter," Jabba said. "I'm not going to kill you."

As Bossk released a nearly imperceptible sigh in relief, Jabba depressed a button on his pipe. "But *he* might," Jabba said, chuckling, as a trapdoor opened beneath the bounty hunter and he dropped to his fate. The rancor hadn't eaten for some days, and it howled in delight at the appearance of a new meal. If Bossk was as tough a warrior as he claimed to be, he would survive.

If not . . . Jabba smiled and dropped another squealing gorg into his maw. If not, no matter. There were plenty of other bounty hunters. Better bounty hunters, who would have no trouble dispensing with human scum like Luke Skywalker or Han Solo. Bounty hunters who would drag Solo to Tatooine and deposit him at Jabba's feet, so he could suffer the fate he deserved.

Torture. Humiliation.

And ultimately, death.

Yes, if Bossk couldn't handle it, there was someone else who could.

Solo had survived long enough; it was time to get the job done. And Jabba had exactly the man to do it. He glowered at his second-in-command. "Get me Boba Fett."